Indian Tea in American Cup

Indian Tea in American Cup

Harish Naval

Ocean Books Pvt. Ltd.

ISO 9001:2015 Publishers

Published by
Ocean Books (P) Ltd.
4/19 Asaf Ali Road,
New Delhi-110 002 (INDIA)
e-mail: oceanbooksindia@gmail.com

ISBN 978-93-92963-10-0
Indian Tea in American Cup
English Translation of 'अमरीकी प्याले में भारतीय चाय'
Novel by Shri Harish Naval

Translation
Dr. Neelam Verma

Edition
First, 2023

Paperback Price
₹ 250.00 (Rupees Two Hundred Fifty only)

Printed at
R-Tech Offset Printers, Delhi

Preface

Many years ago, when I was 10th Class, a series of Satirical conversations between girls and boys was started in 'Neelam', Delhi Magazine. Girls used to write an open letter to boys and boys used to write an open letter to girls. I too participated in it and my letter was awarded the 1st Prize. Many young boys and girls referred to its context and content several times, as a piece of good humour and satire.

My articles had already found space in a magazine, 'Sarvhitkari', published from Dehradun. Its subject matter had moral and religious orientation.

My Hindi school teacher Shri Dharmbhanu 'Sukumar' used to go through both, 'Neelam' and 'Sarvhitkari'. He told me that they were in genre of good satire. He found my expressions quite fluent and original. The writeups in 'Sarvhitkari' where less original.... still should continue with it!

On encouragement from my teacher and mentor I started writing in line with the style of 'Neelam'. I could guess what he meant by 'Original' but was quite ignorant about the word Satire! Then I composed an article in story format. The title was 'Ramchandraji Vs

Shri Krishna'. I tried to portray a Cricket Match between 'Treta Yuga' and 'Dwapar'. The characters of the two eras were depicted as Cricket Stars and described the happenings of the match. My mentor went through it and liked it. In his opinion a contemporary take of mythical characters is acceptable so long as it is restrained. While modernising the narration the expressions should abide by the qualities the characters were acclaimed for. He also felt that my story format was more interesting.

I went ahead and wrote a few more articles even before I became acquainted with the grammar of satire. Around this time the well known story writer Shri Jainendra Kumar happened to visit our school. My mentor told me to present one of my compositions before him. After I read out my article, Jainendraji also commented the same thing. 'You write good satire. Keep it up. It is a tough style.' Then I did not know what 'Satire' is .

While I was in 1st year of my college, my article 'Mr. Commentary Das' was published in a popular Humour cum Satire magazine 'Noke Jhonke' from Agra. I found that the remarks for that article labelled it as 'Satire'. Now I felt inspired and made a conscious effort to understand Satire...and am still doing so (since that time i.e., 1965). In my adolescence I liked to read satirist KrishnaChander and Fikra Tausveen. I found Kanhaiya Lal Kapoor also quite interesting. One day, from a scrap dealer I picked up a Satirical Novel 'Lt. Pigson ki Diary' by Bedhab Banarasi. I read it again and again .I smelld the book had real satire in it!!!

By the time I reached the higher classes in College. I became aware of the 'Satire Guru' status of Harishankar Parsai. The expressions of Parsai touched my deeply.

I had found the Satire I was looking for. Slowly I came to know Parsai more closely. Then how could I stay away from writers like Sharad Joshi, Ravindranath Tyagi, Latif Ghonghi and K.P. Saxena.

In adolescence one is not quite sure about what career to choose. Like a pendulam I was swinging between all possibilities. Sometimes I would be active on stage, sometimes I tried my hand in poetry. In the University I was awarded as the 'Best Story Writer' by Shri Rajendra Yadav. I was perplexed and could not decide what to choose. This was when I heard respected Dr. Vijayendra Snatak explain, during the course of a Writing Workshop, 'Write whatever inspires you from within, but choose one form as your identity...'

Under the influence of Parsai, I chose 'Satire' as my field of creation. At that time, I hardly knew that one day I would not only have the privilege to come close to great Satire writers like Harishankar Parsai, Sharad Joshi, Ravindranath Tyagi, Shrilal Shukla, Latif Ghonghi, Manohar Shyam Joshi, Narendra Kohli and many others, I would also be blessed by them.

In 1975, my satirical article 'Vikramark, Budhiya and Sarai Rohilla' got published in 'sarthak'. I was lucky that it was noticed by Acharya Hazari Prasad Dwivedi. He advised me to avoid populist approach and continue to take satire seriously. I should make all out effort to get into mainstream literary writing.

Since that moment I am striving hard to keep my journey on the right track. Magazines like 'Dharmyug', 'Saptahik Hindustan', 'Sarika', 'Dinman', 'Kadambini' and papers 'Navbharat Times', 'Dainik Hindustan', 'Amar Ujala' and others showed me the way.

In 1987 Bhartiya Jnanpeeth organised a 'Satire Writing Competition'. My manuscript 'Baghpat ke Kharbooje' happened to get declared a winner and was awarded 'Yuva Jnanpeeth Puraskar'.

'Baghpat ke Kharbooje' became a symbol of 'Satire by Young Writers'. It was well received by critics and readers. My name came in limelight just by that competition.... Now I had to shoulder more responsibility. The editors, readers and critics, now had higher expectations from me. I was able to progress and prosper due to a generous association and healthy competition from my contemporary satire writers.

With time, experience enriched, a number of satirical Seminars were being organised within and outside India. I was getting actively involved with them. I worked with a forum by the name 'Madhyam' (conducted by Anup Shrivastava) in Lucknow. It gave me an opportunity to learn and share my views regarding satire and humour. It was in 1991-1992 that such participation made me well versed with prose writing in satire. I had to take gilling queries about its style, status, linguistic aspects, scope and composition skills. The exercise gave me a poignant insight into Hindi prosaic humour and satire. With my limited capability and ideas but unlimited possibilities I tried to create an earnest awareness on them not only in various Indian cities and universities but also in workshops and seminars held in America, England, Canada, Trinidad, Mauritius, Dubai, Sharjah, Cambodia, Japan, Thailand, Bulgaria and many other countries and places.

In Hindi, Comedy and Satire (Hasya and Vyangya) were put together with a mark of hyphen-which made it Hi-fun! Humour is joyful in effect while effect of Satire is sorrowful. Both are tough forms. It is difficult to write something which can create joy through Humour and sorrow through satire. A mature solemn thoughtfulness is not only expected from a satirist, but it is mandatory also. The reader of satire should also be sombre and mature. To get to the last layer of onion can be a tearful experience.

In my opinion both, the humour and satire writers should have a 'sense of humour' and a 'sense of satire'. It's a common observation that when a comical composition has a touch of satire, it become more powerful. More the satire, more the impact. On the other hand, to add a touch of humour to a satire is acceptable to some extent. But going overboard weakens it. For a writer, it is better to improve upon a 'sense of satire'.

A lot is being written in the name of satire. It includes everything from comments, criticism, humour, mockery, a quick review, reporting and likewise. They are in abundance but are not up to the mark. It degrades the level of 'Column Writing' built by Parsai, Joshi, Kittoo... or what is being written by Gyan Chaturvedi. This is why Narendra Kohli categorised Column Writing as 'Pillar Scratching' ('Khambhanochan') Though 'Scratching' is not a satirical expression by any stretch of imagination. Such Column Writing needs to find a category other than Satire.

Ironically, prosaic satire got somewhat side-lined. It stayed unsung by celebrated critics. The satire by Parsai, Joshi, Tyagi and those after them who upheld its status along with magazines like 'Vyangya Yatra' finally made those brilliant thinkers who considered it second rate material, get interested in it. It is a relief to see senior critics like Dr. Namvar Singh, Dr. Nityanand Tiwari, Dr. Vishwanath Tripathi and Dr. Nirmala Jain to recognize the genre of Hindi prosaic satire. Otherwise, the task of reviewing the grammar of satire was being taken up by exclusively those who were satire writers themselves.

So far as my satire writing and vision is concerned, I am still struggling to find satisfactory answers to my dilemmas. Answers do come forth and at times my introspection gives me new insights. I have authored 17 collections of satire and satirical stories, 05 satirical plays and 02 satirical novels and a book on literary criticism of satire.

I am highly obliged to my readers because of whom I have got recognition and encouragement to write better. They have supported me the new ways and brought me to the forefront their feedback is my treasure.

I am thankful to Dr. Neelam Verma, a known literary figure who has translated my Hindi Book in English very well.

My sincere thanks to Mr. Pawan Aggarwal CEO Orient Books and Prabhat Prakashan, New Delhi who has been so kind to get this book published on a very short notice and so beautifully.

I hope that this book will not disappoint the readers.

Best Regards

—Harish Naval

e-mail: harishnaval@gmail.com

Foreword

The cheerful saga of our daily life has harsh undertones which we tend to overlook until they are exposed to us in some form or the other. Here is a series of satire episodes which take a dig at our fake perceptions. In his book 'Indian Tea in American Cup' Harish Naval stirs up myriad shades of human emotions. As an accomplished satirist, he carefully scratches the superficial sheen to unearth the underlying dark mosaic of human nature.

Naval tackles every aspect of our morality and ethics. Our National Ethos, Religious Tantrums, Political Gimmicks, Educational Misadventures or Social Rituals are all under his probing eyes. He mercilessly delves into each and every corner of our psyche and questions the sincerity of our consciousness. Stretching us much beyond our comfort zones is what makes his satire hard-hitting without being vulgar.

The curtain raiser for the series makes a direct hit at our religious beliefs. When one becomes illogical about one's own faith, these beliefs become overbearing. Listening to even a school prayer can create a hypothetical web of queries in the mind of grown-ups. While innocent kids easily grasp what is implied, mature minds fail to connect to it. Then there is light at the end of the dark tunnel—

'How will I find a Virtuous Way...I need to hold on to The Merciful within me, but how...'

Even after brewing deep, everything fizzles out like a storm in a teacup...

Then there is an account of hollow promises of our Glorious National Heritage. While everyone wants to share the lime light of the new found 'Autonomy', no one is accountable for the 'sinking boat'!

We have to look for answers within ourselves—

'... Could the Nation that was enthralled by inspiring tales of martyrdom, achieve Independence in true spirit?'

Naval next takes on the misadventures in our education system which are propelled by the likes of highly qualified Dr. Bhatia. Dilemma of a Hindi Professor who looks forward to making some quick bucks by agreeing to do marking for English Board answer sheets is a highly 'confidential' matter. Naval, who himself is a seasoned academician, is clever enough not to let Dr. Bhatia utter the last sentence—'I am an honest and responsible person!'

Naval then turns to the trench around Red Fort. It actually represents the out of reach stature of our leaders who want to be regarded as symbols of National pride and dignity. One wonders, how well are they connected to the people of the country...

Naval then shifts his focus to a hilarious scenario where a hospital management wants to allure patients by making it an entertainment hot spot. The doctors are in splits as Naval's out of the world ideas are narrated to them... How much more seriously can you take a mockery...! The puns are almost hysterical.

According to Naval, earning respect is no longer about raising your own self. Actually, it's about making others trip and fall. Going from 'Touch the feet dramatics' to 'Foot Choppers' and 'Floor movers', Naval muses in the thoughts of true respect and regard people had for their genuine masters in the era gone by.

In the quest for Ultimate Yoga, new Asana and Kriya are being constantly unearthed by the mystics. Naval moves away from Laughter the Best Medicine or Laughter Yoga. He introduces us to Yoga Guru Krandananda, who turns everything upside down.

When Guruji developed and demonstrated 'Tears of Malice Yoga Kriya', the followers forgot to clap in applause. 'Instead, they had a Cry—Outburst and there was a mad-rush to get to touch the feet of revered Guruji.'

Naval takes us from 'Honesty is the best policy to Honesty is a sample of stupidity...' He brings out the glaring contrast between the stigma attached to our Bhartiya identity and the honour enjoyed by self- respecting NRI diaspora. The satire is a total catharsis...

Naval then rakes up the long-standing battle between the system and the governance and goes on to strip the obsolete dogmas we have been carrying on for ages. We become weary of these regressive traditions but do not dare to get rid of them. Can we reinvent our social values in tandem with the time we live in?

'May Time be our saviour'

There is a lot of bull-shit our countryside is full of. To clean this, mammoth efforts are planned but no one comes out to take the bull by the horns. More than funds and resources, what it needs is motivation...So National

Disaster management at grass-root level remains stubbornly stagnant.

Removing a dead cat from college premises becomes an encounter of another kind where the principal has no option but to run for his life...literally!

Naval sees a catastrophy waiting to happen when Gandhi's statute needs a wash. Just the mention of it opens a Pandora Box and everything goes wrong in every possible way.

Taking a dig at digital world Naval brings forth the debacle of real world in its tussle with the overpowering virtual avatars.

'Let's drop the falling flag of our consciousness and take a Selfie of the Self-Within.'

Contemplation upon Deities is a common practice in Hindu culture. As Naval observes them from the mundane world we live in, he concludes—

'Deities never let their feet touch the ground.'

We can't agree more.

Revealing the super-human powers of the symbols of Mighty Divinities like Hanuman and Bheem, Naval draws a similarity between them and our contemporary heroes as we see them appearing around us in various cinematic forms, 'Hanuman and Bheem standing in some corner... are watching it all with tearful eyes and folded hands.'

The third trip of a SIL to his in-law's house is an educational expedition. The welcome chants are unceremoniously replaced by abusive humour. If the thought of excusing oneself on any pretext rises, the all-knowing wife spoils it—'Oh I understand everything... there you would just loiter around in the neighbourhood instead of making any notes....'

An hilarious encounter with Aunt Toshi and her 'Billo Rani' song is a peppy devotional take on scrupulous Divine Love gone wrong.

Going overboard with the definition of 'Poverty-Line 'draws a blank. One wonders who created this myth of 'Being Poor' when no poor can be found anywhere.

Debate over India Vs Bharata is going on perpetually in one form or the other. Naval is in good command while going through this hot topic The daring satirist in him does not hesitate to hit below the belt when Chachaji declares, 'My dear, you are a college professor and teach so many things....I had an impression that you are highly intelligent but....!' This take on the relevance of our Independence Day celebrations is what goes on in the mind of confused Indian citizens.

Naval, then targets a political menace called Rally. Why the hell are they held and what do they achieve? Rally is a popular mode of asserting political dissent, usually over trivial issues. Besides the relevance or irrelevance of this 'Fifth Pillar'...the Rallies actually nurture and invigorate the wealth of Media Houses. Without Rallies, their TRP will nosedive and they will become flop -shows. Here Naval does not hesitate to call a spade, a spade!

In our life Awards have become an essential commodity, whatever the field. Award functions add sheen to our otherwise lack lustre existence. Naval recreates the phenomenal rise of Award functions with tongue in cheek observation—'...If you feel something is turning in you... realise, your soul is yearning for an Award and Applaud... by hook or by crook find an Award and become famous.'

Then 'It's your destiny and karma that how many columns news you can be...'

Horrors of another kind are waiting to ring in 'Me Too' alarm bells. It's a fad to be included in this process of being dis-robed and dis-honoured. This new found crisis is a witty exposure of a morally sick society.

'We are not considered a celebrity but might be there is a high-profile lady who will disclose our past lewd behaviour and thereby make us a celebrity.'

In this statement Naval excels himself as deceptively innocuous prototype of uninhibited satire!

Drawing parallels between the style of Arabic Folklore and gruesome Gulf-War through a Pehalwan's Puppy brings home all the missing links without raising a finger...

The book ends with a luxurious satire drama - University Shraadh Season. Admission days are when College Professors are revered like the crows during Shraadh season. The screenplay is an outright melodrama depicted with full malice towards 'expecting without deserving' college aspirants.

Indian Tea in American Cup show cases the chic narrative style, Naval has crafted for himself. I am sure this book will give readers a different perspective of the world they live in.

Every sip from Indian Tea in American Cup brings a crackling taste of human nature.

Congratulations to Harish Naval for his brilliant sarcasm.

—Dr. Neelam Verma

Contents

1
Indian Tea in American Cup

Four wrought iron chairs in white, set around a white table, adorn the courtyard of my home. This is where I start my day. The spot has lush green plants spread around and there is a Play School in the neighbourhood.

Over here I settle down after my morning walk and prepare basil green tea in my American tea cup. Around this time the morning prayer starts at the school. As I sip my tea I get to hear the Prayer-Song coming from the school loudspeakers. I had heard the melodious words several decades ago, complete with visuals in a movie. I happened to hear it at several other occasions. Since the time I have been staying here, I hear them daily and contemplate upon them. It stirs my soul with melancholy. The words are—

'O Merciful, give us strength,
firm in our faith we stay;
we never ever falter even by mistake,
while we tread the virtuous way!'

I know, just like me, several people must have heard this 'Prayer.' They must be listening to it in schools and temples every day. Just like me, they might have even contemplated upon it. Is it possible that 'The Merciful' can give such a strength? If he can, then how? What should be done by us to get such an amazing strength which will not let our faith falter? An ordinary person like me finds it faltering daily. How can I become strong enough? Who else can give me the strength, if not 'The Merciful'?

'Merciful' means God! Who is God? God, the One with all the astounding powers, the One who decides our fate... the Grand Master who can turn a zero into a hero and a hero into a zero...Where can He be found? How can He gift us such a strength?

This sequential contemplation continues from one end to the other till the whole of Indian green tea from the American tea cup is sipped away. Though this trail of thoughts is not hurdle free but it is smooth enough. Who is worthy to be God? I start pondering over the mythological context which considers Brahma, Vishnu and Mahesh to be bestowed upon with Godly characteristics.

Brahma created the universe, created us all. He could have made our heart full of the necessary strength but it is doubtful if his own heart was strong enough. He, who abducted his own daughter, indicates how weak His own heart is!

Should I pray to God Vishnu who is resting in the lap of Sheshnag floating in the Ocean of Milk. As a caretaker of whole of the universe, He himself is already exhausted. Goddess Lakshmi is pressing his tired feet. How can I place my request in front of a tired God, there are millions of people in the waiting, when will He hear me? Will I even stay alive till that time? Should I look up to God Shiva? He is easy to please. To begin with he was so innocent that he blessed all seekers in no time. But since the time he saved himself from the clutches of

Bhasmasur, He became smarter. I am skeptical if it will be possible for Shiva absorbed in deep Samadhi to come out of His trance and strengthen my heart.

Should I seek the grace of Maryada Purushottam Rama? But here also I am not really hopeful. The prayer says, 'never ever falter.' How can Rama assure this? His own confidence in Sita's purity was so flimsy that He asked for her to give 'Agni-Pariksha'! In due course He even exiled her to forest at a time when she was pregnant...! How do I expect any strength from Lila Purushottam Krishna whose own life was full of ambiguities and contradictions. His own confidence was so badly shaken that He ran away from the battlefield and took shelter in the ocean city of Dwarika!

I am contemplating upon various contemporary saints, learned men, realised souls whose Godly stories I have heard for so long...their images move across my mind like a film. Side by side their weaknesses also come to the forefront...witnessed by millions and trillions of their devotees! Then who really is 'The Merciful?' The question challenges me again and again.

Can those who frame the constitution or those who rule us be called 'The Merciful?' How do I find the 'virtuous' way? Whom do I ask? I dive into the deep pond of introspection. Virtuous way, means the path of truthfulness, the path of honesty...I know how risky the path is. If I work honestly, I will be transferred. If I don't bribe, everything will come to a screeching halt, nothing will move...if I do not indulge in flattery, I will sink, truthfulness will ruin me...I have seen how injustice challenges those who are sincere!

How will I find 'Virtuous way?'...So many values have

become worthless. Those who found the way up with our support, have conspired against us, after several of those who rise to fame leave no efforts unturned to bring us shame. They become so rude that they just give us a cold shoulder. We don't matter to them anymore. Exposing them or going against them is simply suicidal.

Neither the green tea nor the lush greenery around me could provide any succour. It became difficult to differentiate whether the prayer-song was churning me or was it the other way round! Great thinkers like Buddha, Mahavir and Vivekananda provide me the secret to awaken my wisdom...' Be your own light,' I start seeing 'light!' It dawns upon me that to strengthen my faith, I need to be 'The Merciful' myself. I get enlightened-I introspect-I see clearly that all virtues are lying shattered, while the vices are glittering bright...Truthfulness is finding veils to hide itself while the 'fake' market is in full bloom. It's hot and raving mad to suck it all.

I need to hold on to 'The Merciful 'within me, on my own, but how? Would it be possible without 'The Merciful' helping me from outside? Will I have to fight this battle alone? My battle with my own self? If I wish to rise, will I have to be 'The Merciful' myself? That means, I will have to sing the Prayer-Song, to myself, not to anyone else...but how?

As I am sinking in my thoughts, my better half places the school bag of my son on the round table and orders me, 'Go, drop Munnu at school bus stop.'

'So early?' I argue meekly.

She answers, 'You haven't finished his homework. First complete it, then drop him.'

Words of my wife are more powerful than the Prayer

Song...my thoughts drift away from the 'faith I was trying to build up. I focus upon completing Munnu's homework.

My Indian ideology is shattered to pieces. I crave for another American cup of Green Tea before I can faithfully complete Munnu's homework.

□

2
Our Autonomy

It was midnight in 1947 when our own government came to power. We were no longer in the category of slaves. Now where do slaves go after they are set free? This was a big dilemma facing the country as well as the rulers. They solved it by assuming that they had got the full and final ownership rights of the country. By courtesy of Mahatma and other known and unknown revolutionaries they got rid of the shackles that were severed at last. They jostled together to seize the objective they were dying to achieve. It was irrelevant whether they ever lived for it or not...

It was presumed that everything belonged to us. The new dogma was that in autonomy, everything is 'auto', i.e., self-owned. De facto, when everything is apparently your own, nothing really belongs to you! Our propagators led by example. Like Eklavya we became their unequivocal disciples and quickly learnt that the word 'autonomy' implies 'common property.' It was realised much later that whatever is 'common,' belongs to no one. The passage to ten flats is usually without light because no single person is accountable for it.

Getting 'autonomy' was like getting Crowned the

King of England. Each one of us believed himself to be the King! Imagine the state of affairs of England with trillions of Kings. What did those Kings do? We had a patriotic song that said, 'We have saved our boat from a storm in the ocean, Oh dear children, take care of this Nation!' But children had become Kings. Where and what did these Kings take care of?

The bread was snatched from the hands that sowed the seeds, there was loot in name of business, cut-money in name of making money, everything slipped downhill towards bankruptcy!

What did we do to the 'autonomy' for which thousands of our zealous nationalists sacrificed their comforts and youth? We did not hesitate to auction it in an open market. Could the nation that was enthralled for centuries by the inspiring tales of martyrdom, achieve Independence in true spirit? Over the years, the successors of those in power, crushed the Democratic System time and again.

The princely states and privy purses were abolished. The princely states of neo-influential genre bloomed and flourished. Soon 'khadi,' 'topi' and 'neta' found different meanings. From ordinary they became the symbols of extraordinary.

The discreet movement to convert black money power to white vote power, crucified the ethics of a fair political system. Crumbling between the power of money and power of vote, stood the one who though inconsequential, was most elated on achieving the dream called 'autonomy.' Raising the slogans of 'Jai Hind' in front of the Red Parapet, this 'common man emptied his pockets in lieu of more and more slogans.

How irrational was this 'autonomy' where the boatman was himself bent upon sinking the boat. The house was set aflame by the lamps meant to light it up. Our centuries old cultural heritage was getting reduced to ashes. The Neo-rich culture was in vogue. These affluent prince and princesses invented unique ways to glorify prosperity.

Thankfully, whistle blowers too swung into action and marred the sinister designs of these dupers. Colours of 'Topi' changed. Most of the colours faded off. However, some bright rainbow colours could also be spotted. There was hope that spring will not be far away.

At the moment, there is a possibility of 'autonomy' being ours for real. This reality will become real only when we, as well as those up the ladder, become 'truthful' and stay away from falsehood.

Let's hope for such an 'autonomy' one day.

□

3

Honesty@Responsibility.Com

Board examinations were over and it was now the season of checking the answer sheets. The English question paper had been set by me, so the job of being the Chief Examiner was entrusted to me. 28 teachers of various schools were functioning as examiners under my supervision. The teachers who teach the subject in the school for years together rarely get the opportunity to set the question paper. The less experienced college professors like me are given the charge of setting the School Board examination papers-this was apparently absurd, but was the accepted norm. Before calling the 28 teachers for discussion, it was imperative for me to know what the exact answers were supposed to be and what were the criteria to be considered while examining the answers. I was engrossed in scrutinizing these details and was feeling edgy about it. Children of my known contacts who studied in the same class had gone away on holiday after completing their exams. I was not able to get from them an idea about the mental state of those students, and the anxieties they face while framing the answers. I had to figure out on my own and I wanted the examiners to follow the necessary instructions.

At this crucial time my school classmate Dr. Vijay Kumar Bhatia called me up. He wanted me to meet him alone for something urgent. He planned to reach me in an hour once I told him that my wife had gone to see her parents and I was alone at home.

In about an hour, Dr. Vijay Kumar Bhatia dashed into my study, fully loaded. Loaded, because he carried Tikki-Samosa along with my favourite sweets from Kamla Nagar market and also a bundle of papers. Dr. Bhatia teaches Hindi in a college. We studied together in a Daryaganj school. I was in English debate team while he was in Hindi debate team. I couldn't learn good Hindi from him while he couldn't learn good English from me. He could not converse with anyone in proper English. Whenever I told him to practice talking to me in English, he reasoned that so many great Hindi writer professors did not know English but were famous and honoured. I failed to understand his logic behind this excuse.

After relishing samosas, tikki and gajerela, I raised an inquisitive glance at Dr. Bhatia. Suddenly his glowing face looked pale. He came closer to me and muttered, 'Dear, you are my friend for twenty years. Please help me. I am carrying a heavy burden of responsibilities-please reduce my burden! You are already checking the English literature papers. I have been asked to check English language papers. Please help me.' I was taken aback. 'Dr. Bhatia, you have to check English language papers? But why? How come you didn't get Hindi papers to check?'

'Yes Dear, I got them. I checked them and deposited them with the Board. Now I have received the English papers.' He replied.

'But how have these papers come to you? You are...!'

'You mean that when I am a Hindi professor, how can I possibly get these?' He said, 'Dear, I told you it's the burden of responsibility. I am duty bound to check these papers. I have to fulfil this. I am an honest and responsible person; you know quite well.'

'But according to the rules and regulations these papers should not have come to you. Didn't the board ask you to fill the Consent Form? I can't really understand this. Only thing I understand is that the one who hardly ever offers a cup of tea, why has he today got me samosa tikki!' I said with a hint of disgust in my voice.

Dr. Bhatia spoke like a gentleman, 'Dear, I received the Consent Form. A big brown envelope. The standard one that comes from Board office. I opened it. There was a request letter for me to check English language paper. I felt honoured and accepted it. Wrote 'Yes' and returned the Consent Form. The office has sent me this bundle of six hundred and seventy-six answer sheets,' saying this he pointed towards the bundle he carried.

I asked 'With the Consent Form there is an attached proforma. You have to fill your qualifications in it. You must have given correct information in it.'

'What are you saying Dear? I am an honest and responsible professor...I filled the proforma correctly and mentioned my qualifications...M.A., Ph-D. In my address I mentioned clearly, Dr. Vijay Kumar Bhatia, Hindi Reader...' he answered.

I argued trying to contradict him, 'But why did you accept it? You knew you received it by mistake. You could have consulted someone, asked someone, might be there was someone else by the same name.'

'Dear, how could I ask anyone? I had opened up

the envelope. It was marked 'Confidential.' Now the confidential information can't be shared publically. One has to safeguard secrecy of the matter.'

'Are you sure? Was it in your name?' I was about to have a blast.

'Yes, Dear, yes...it was in my name only. It was delivered at my college address. The peon Rampyara handed it over to me. I opened it and filled the correct information in the form. Now when Board had no objection, why you...you are showing resentment? Board office also has honest and responsible staff...they have sent these English papers after evaluating all the points. Had they not sent, I would not have come to you' he said getting agitated.

'Oh, my friend, you should not have accepted the request. What was the need to do so? You knew it was wrong.' I spoke.

'But where have I gone wrong? I didn't go to Board office to get these English papers. They requested, I accepted. They wanted me to keep it confidential, I abided by their orders. Now comes the question of need. Dear, I am always in need. I have not studied English like you. I am living in a rented accommodation for eleven years... children go to public school; parents stay with me. Two of my sisters are still to be married off. A teacher has no extra source of income. I am a Hindi teacher. A subject, for which no one needs a tutor. Its unlike your English tuitions.'

'Whatever extra income I can have Dear, is through these papers and invigilation duties during these Examination days. Then why should I not have accepted it? There's nothing wrong in it. It's so honourable.'

I felt that instead of saying anything else I should help him. He kept the English question paper and the list of instructions he had received from the head examiner in front of me. The papers had to be checked accordingly.

I proposed to Bhatia, if I should check the papers. His answer in the cover of honesty and responsibility was that he preferred to do his job himself. It's definitely wrong to get someone else work for you.

I made a sincere effort to tell him the process of examining and make him understand. Though I am not sure how much he really understood. From the answer sheets he carried in the bundle, I read out a few and explained the marking strategy. He left gratefully and said,' Dear, I will be fair in my judgement and will remember you always. I heard you have taken study leave for two years and will be leaving for London. That's really great. You studied English while in India. I have PhD in Hindi. Be happy wherever you are. Here or in London. We are always going to be in India.'

As he left, he bid me farewell in English with a 'Bye Bye'.

Time passed slowly and steadily at its own pace. I finished my education from London University and returned. I joined college and life was back in its set pattern. On College Convocation Day, I suddenly happened to meet Dr. Vijay Kumar Bhatia. He was exhilarated on seeing me. He gave me a warm hug and said 'Oh Dear, you look all the more handsome. You have returned from London. A treat is due.'

I offered him to accompany me for a cup of coffee in the coffee house. While having coffee and enjoying a burger along with it, we had much to gossip about. I recollected the past episode and asked, 'tell me Bhatia, what happened to the English papers you once got. Did it all go well?'

'Yes Dear! It went perfectly fine. Most of the students got mediocre marks. Only those failed who had given answers of just one or two questions...I passed all the others. My result was very good. Board officers were also very happy. You gave me practical tips, and

Dear! I got a generous Extra income too.'

'So now you must be checking Hindi papers!' I commented with a smile.

He said, 'Of course I do. But side by side I also check English papers.'

I was about to lose my senses, 'You do? But how?'

'Dear, you know very well that whenever Board office accepts someone as an examiner, the responsibility is for three years, if everything else is all right. So now this is my third year and I am thoroughly enjoying, as you know...'

...I cut short his sentence 'I am an honest and responsible person!'

Whatever had to be lost, was lost!

☐

4
Red Fort and a Trench

India is a country dominated by Forts. All the foreign tourists making a trip to prominent Indian cities, make sure to visit the Forts nearby. These Forts have become a major tourist attraction. They have been standing as relentless guards for ages. The enthusiastic Tour Guides who grow up in the shadows of these Forts, are well versed to narrate the details of their grandeur, majesty and the half-baked historical tales associated with them.

Have you ever given a thought to the similarities between our Forts and Leaders? The aura of grandeur that Leaders exude, sometimes surpasses the Forts!

These Leaders symbolize ability to withstand all shocks and challenges. Whatever they do for themselves is actually in favour of nation and come what may, their own stability is absolutely unshakable...their economics thrive on credit. Of course, on account of the Nation...their glorious credentials and historical memoirs are narrated with a lot of frills by their sycophant guides. Their invisible flags can be felt fluttering triumphantly, much higher than the visible flags hoisted on the Forts...

...You must have been to several Forts. Delhi is the pride of India and The Red Fort is Delhi's 'Mark of Identification.' You too must have seen it.

When viewed from a distance, The Red Fort gives an extremely imposing look, as if it's inviting you to come nearer. There is a trench around it, which remains hidden... Such a trench surrounds every Fort. Our glorious Leaders are also surrounded by a similar trench...the bigger and deeper the trench, higher the stature of the Leader. From far off such a leader appears to be well grounded and connected to the people of the country but as soon as you go closer to him, you just find him out of reach. You must beware of the 'trench' around him, otherwise you are bound to slip into it, before you realize...

Amen!

□

5
Hospi—Entertainment

It was around 9.30 at night. I signalled my attendant and friend Narender to switch off the light. As soon as lights were out, I stretched out myself from half reclined posture and tried to sleep off. Before I could do so, I was surprised to hear the door buzzer. Nurses had left after winding up their duty. Nothing more had to be done... now I had to signal Narender. I called him and requested him to put on the lights and open the door.

When the door opened, a well-dressed gentleman with a file in his hand walked in. I took him to be a doctor. I got back to half-reclined posture like a mouse so that he could check me up. The gentleman said softly, 'Please excuse me Sir, I was walking towards your room when the lights were put off. I pressed the buzzer because I had to meet you urgently.'

As soon as he addressed me as 'Sir 'I realised that he was not a doctor. Rather we address a doctor as 'Sir.' Then who is he and why has he come to see me?

Reading the curious expressions rolling over my face, he drew closer and said, 'Sir I am from Entertainment Department-to provide some amusement to patients in hospital. I had to consult you urgently...Dr. Sonal Gupta had instructed me to see you and I had to comply her orders today itself.'

His words were like a bitter pill but the name of Dr. Sonal Gupta made it sweet.

'Sure, how can I be of help? What did Dr. Sonal Gupta say?'

'Sir, tomorrow there is a board meeting to discuss various ways to entertain the patients. Dr. Gupta told me that in Room No. 403 of Neurosurgery ward a writer journalist has been admitted...Take new entertainment ideas from him. He will be able to tell better.'

Now his face had many queries rolling over it with tints of exclamatory expressions...for a few moments I went into a trance. As I came back to my senses, I told Narender to offer him a chair.

Now the chair was occupied by the Entertainment Department representative Sofa-cum-Bed by the attendant and on the royal bed was seated-'My Majesty.' The new comer's face was under the vivid glare of the Divine glowing lampshade of Room No. 403 in that super speciality hospital. In the amazing light effects, novel ideas flashed through my mind.

I had a sip of water and urged my speech to rise to the occasion. Narender too was wide awake and the officer opened his file and got prepared. He spread a fresh sheet of paper on the file and got ready with his pen...He asked in all attentiveness, 'Yes Sir, what can the ideas be?'

I got ready with my speaking skills and asked, 'Oh, what do you call the girls draped in short dresses, who dance on the cricket ground?'

Narender and the officer answered in chorus, 'Cheer Girls!'

'Yes, Cheer Girls! Good! Note down idea number one, 'Book Cheer Girls for Hospi-Entertainment!'

The officer looked stunned. Narender had a ray of hope gleaming in his eyes.

'Sir, how can we do this? How many 'Cheer Girls' will be there? How will they come? What will they do? Who will get them and from where? The officer was lost in a smog of queries.

'You know there is cricket match going on in the Delhi Firozshah Kotla Ground. Cheer Girls are already there. They can be contacted!'

'They are all foreigners and will charge us heavily. We need them for whole of the hospital, so we will have to book them in a large number.' The officer gave a lost look at his waves of confusion. I told him in a well-controlled voice, 'Well, you will need only three of them.'

'Only three Cheer Girls? Sir, we have fourteen wards!!!' He jumped into the waves.

I made an attempt to retrieve him, 'Send them to each of the wards for twenty minutes. One Cheer Girl should go to each patient's room and dance for three minutes to entertain him.'

'Sir, just three minutes? Three minutes is...'

I interrupted him before he could complete his sentence, 'A film song entertains us a lot in three minutes. Cheer Girl can go again to the same patient to entertain him, if time allows. Not all rooms belong to a single patient. Some rooms have two, some have four while some have even eight patients.'

The officer looked impressed. He made some notes and asked, 'Sir, from where do we make their payments?'

I took a deep breath,' It's a big hospital and is making

good money. Tell the Board to impose P.E.T. It will help you meet the expenses and also generate additional revenue.'

'Sir, what is P.E.T.?'

'Patient Entertainment Tax.' I could feel my collars were turning up. I gazed towards Narender. He was trying hard to control his laughter.

'Yes Sir, it's a damn good idea. That's why Dr. Gupta has sent me to consult you. You are so right Sir. Increasing the bill by half a percent raises our revenue by millions. Now how to book Cheer Girls. The Board members would like to know tomorrow.'

I spoke, 'Contact Indian Cricket Control Board. Send them an official letter from here. You should not approach them alone. Take a couple of lady doctors along. The girls need money. Your accountant with cash in hand should also accompany you.'

'Sir, I would present all these details in the Board Meeting tomorrow-let's see! But this is only one idea. Sir please, I need some more ideas...' He made a modest request.

Officer's serious humility was noticed by Narender. He managed to suppress the naughty expressions in his eyes and addressed me, 'Your idea is so brilliant! This will bring laurels to the hospital as well as this officer. You must be having many more ideas. Please give him. After all, he has been sent by Dr. Sonal Gupta!'

I took a pause for a couple of minutes. Then spoke out 'Look Narender, I do have another idea.'

'Please share!' I could sense the amusement Narender was feeling.

'Make a note of it...Idea number two!' I spoke to the officer.

'Yes Sir, I am ready!'

'See, this special mattress on my bed has its machine over here, on the arm of the bed. When we switch it on, the water in the mattress is set to motion...'

'Yes Sir. This is to protect against bed sores. Shall I switch it on?' The officer asked.

'No but my idea is connected to it. The HD TV on the front wall can be connected to it...the music played on the TV will pass through this mattress and its water will flow in its rhythm...just imagine, how much relaxation it will give to the patient. The water current will dance on the tunes being played, may it be classical, pop, light music, folk, sufi or a gazal...'

'Wow, that would be fantastic. 'The officer jumped with joy. 'Sir, there would be a choice of Hindi, English, Bengali, Marathi channels to be played. The patient would get in contact with the musical waves of the State he is from. It won't cost us much. We can get the leads from Karol Bagh market...we can provide them for the beds where these mattresses are being used. That's too good.' He was obviously thrilled. Narender had to struggle to keep his laughter under control. In the process tears were about to roll down his cheeks.

I took some water and rested till the officer noted it all.

'Sir, please give another powerful idea...similar to this!' The officer requested.

Narender said, 'Why not? Our Sir is a powerhouse of ideas. He will surely pull out some more for you. A minimum of three must be there...Trinity of Brahma, Vishnu and Mahesh. Please Sir, give another idea.'

I was now ready with more. The officer was all ears, with open pen and mouth.

Narender was staring at me, expectantly. 'This too is tech-savvy. Note down 'Idea Number Three. This is a bright and luminous idea. The hospital will need trails of lights with tiny bulbs. Have you seen such lights?'

'Yes Sir, the Chinese lights. My uncle gifted me this Diwali. They glitter like fire-flies 'The officer opened up his Google enriched vocabulary to show off.

'These lights are also to be connected to the mattress. This is SLW...Sound Light Water idea. Phillips brand was the first one to invent it. SLW.'

'Yes Sir, my father told me that his first radio was from Phillips brand. They also make tubelights and bulbs. Google was refreshing its info.'

'Get these Chinese light trails and arrange them around the beds with water mattresses. Just connect them to this arm-machine...that's it!'

'But how will this work?' Narender got confused.

'Oh yes, the Illumination of Diwali on the bed...but I don't know how to explain the Board members tomorrow. The entertainment officer was in a mess.'

'You couldn't understand? Use your own brain also. With TV music, the water in the mattress will move rhythmically and the Chinese lights go off and on. Imagine how entertaining this would be to the patient. In all this light, music and water he is sure to forget his illness.'

The officer sprang with happiness and Narender was full of pride. The officer noted down something and said, 'Sir, this idea can be labelled as JTP? 'Jal-Tarang-Prakash?' His collars were turning up.

Narender repeated after him, 'JTP will be more famous than GST. Not only a first in Delhi, it will be a first in India.'

'Sir, why not a first in the whole world?' The officer muttered.

My words impressed him, 'First in the universe. Nothing like this has ever happened in whole of the Cosmos. Such ideas have never been discussed before.'

The officer got up, packed up his files and secured his pen in his pocket. He dashed towards the door.

'Just a moment, Mr. Officer 'I called upon him dogmatically. 'Be seated. Open your file and take a note of-Idea number four. This is mandatory.'

The officer was back on his seat. He opened his file, snapped the pen out of his pocket and got ready to write. He gazed at me with a high expectation. Narender was also perplexed and wondered what next. He had palpated seriousness in my tone.

'Note it down right away...Number four-Never ever ring the buzzer of a patient's room, if the lights are off.' Saying this I slipped into the bed.

Narender told me later, how the officer kept staring at me in disbelief. Then whispered an apology 'Sorry, Sir, so sorry!' and walked away.

As soon as the officer was out, Narender could open up the hearty laughter he had held up for nearly forty minutes. As he switched off lights, he just managed to say, 'Oh Dear, you are impossible...'

Next morning was the regular hospital 'Nursing Morning.' There was usual hustle and bustle. Morning tea was served. Narender reorganised the Sofa cum Bed and said, 'Last night was a blast. I was talking about the Trinity of Brahma, Vishnu and Mahesh and that moron was literally noting down everything.'

We had a lot to gossip over the tea and listening to

the LED TV in High Definition. We could even hear the imaginary music from the bed-machine and see the glittery world of Chinese lights going off and on.

The daily routine started. Nurses came to collect the blood samples. The Physiotherapist made me have a walk around the ward. I had my breakfast. New investigations chart was pasted over my bedside records. Thermometer and Blood

Pressure equipment were put to appropriate usage.

Now we waited for the team of doctors coming for the rounds. Dr. Sonal Gupta was a part of the team...I groomed myself adequately and gazed at the door in anticipation. Narender was all dressed up to leave after finishing his daily chores. His substitute attendant Omar Shah was about to arrive.

...We suddenly felt a wave gushed towards the door. The team of doctors came up to the door and then went away. Myself and Narender got alarmed. Narender walked up to the door. He could see the doctors again making their way towards our door. The doctors who usually came with serious looks, wearing white coats and necklace of stethoscope were rolling in laughter...the ward boys and sisters standing outside the door looked outrightly curious.

Doctors in laughing mode, assembled around my bed. I greeted them and asked what was it all about, there was Board meeting also. Overwhelmed with their laughter, they were in no mood to answer me. One of the doctors remarked 'Please ask Dr. Sonal. She is our head. She will answer you.'

Dr. Sonal controlled her laughing spell and said, 'We are coming from the Board meeting. We were open to your ideas regarding Hospi-Entertainment. The way the officer who visited you narrated your ideas, we could not decide whether to cry or to laugh. The officer was bent upon taking me to Cricket ground to book the Cheer Girls, right away. He was giving details of various Chinese lights to Dr. Manish to go to the market and buy them. The Board meeting was on and we had to look serious... but not anymore...Actually Chairman Sir has asked us to meet you once and discuss it and then put the ideas into action but his PA hasn't turned up today. He is at the Cricket ground to watch the match...' saying this she was again in a fit of laughter. She took a pause and said 'Your Cheer Girls are also in the Cricket ground...'

I acted to listen to her earnestly and advised, 'Let the Chairman talk to his PA on phone and talk to the Cheer Girls. At least some work can start on one of the ideas...'

Without giving any response and without looking at the reports Dr. Sonal gave me an understanding nod and left with the team of doctors. Omar Shah was already waiting outside. He entered the room and asked, 'Is it all good? How are the reports?'

Narender replied as he walked out of the door, 'Omar, the report shows PET and JTP. For his treatment CG, means Cheer Girls are coming over. 'Before leaving he also gave an understanding nod.

Omar found his words strange and muttered 'Narender makes me go mad!'

Now, how could I tell who was making it a mad house...!

□

6
Respect—My Foot

One wonders at the traditional way of demonstration of respect by touching the feet of another person. It is considered a token of social mannerism. A Yogic movement is performed in which a person bends forward to touch the feet of the one to whom he intends to offer his salutation. The process looks more like touching the shoes or the slippers instead of feet and becomes a cultural stroking of 'Footwear.' It is questionable if even that is achieved. The person offering his regards hardly reaches up to the knees of the recipient. This can rather be termed 'Touch the Knee!' Many youngsters don't care to take their lotus-hands that far either. They complete the formality of paying their respect by making a ceremonial forward bend, with extended arms. In the process their hands stay about a foot away and parallel to the waistline of the recipient. This in cultural terms can be termed as 'Touch the Feet Dramatics!'

In this mortal world there is a rare breed that literally goes down to touch the feet or the footwear and a special variety performs it diligently, again and again. They are actually 'Foot Choppers.' They meticulously chop the feet of their guru, father, brother and other similar class of people. In due course they evolve into MLAs, MPs and other prestigious parliamentary capacities.

There are some really religious ones. They do not chop the feet of those they hold in high esteem. They tirelessly touch the revered feet, even rub their forehead on the toes. They bring no harm to the feet but their efforts manage to move the floor under the feet they touch. The respected lot is able to realise what has gone wrong, only after they trip and fall. These expert 'Floor Movers' are usually near and dear relatives like son, daughter-in-law, son-in-law and other similar loved ones.

Gone is the era when those who touched the feet, took care that the feet of their respected masters never touched the ground. Their heaven was at their feet. Ironically, at present these very masters are considered no better than a used slipper. Those who touch the feet, as well as those who get them touched with sattwic purity at heart, are on way to extinction. Those who touch the feet with sheer devotion, have another point of view. They believe that one should touch feet of only those persons whose character is really worthy of it. Now friends, just think if it is ever possible to come across such honourable human beings?

□

7
Cry Yoga Camp

Locals were at a loss to see this topic on the poster. The Notice Board usually had casual posters of 'Laughter Yoga Camp.' Its replacement by this 'Cry Yoga Camp' was a mind-boggling piece of information.

The Camp was going to discuss the benefits of crying and shedding tears. It was underlined four times that crying is a form of Yoga Practice and more effective than Laughter Yoga. Chimanbhai, the honourable president of the locality captured the gist of the poster and planned a meeting of the action committee. It was unanimously decided that the morning session of Laughter Yoga held in the neighbouring park would be replaced by 'Cry Yoga Camp.' If found to be helpful, it would be made a regular feature.

The 'Cry Yoga Guru' was informed and the sessions were scheduled to commence from the coming Monday. Those who came to attend the inaugural programme were instructed by the Yoga Guru that all participants would loudly cry instead of laughing. There would be no sound of 'Hahaha.' The sound would be deep painful shrieks of wailing with 'Oohoo...Oohoo.'

The first trial session of Cry Yoga was a let-down. The

participants tried to make crying noises but they lacked the stereophonic punch of a grieving catastrophe. The Cry Yoga Guru then led by example. He demonstrated the craft of top notch crying and justified his worthy name...the atmosphere thundered with human cries. Overwhelming howls were well perceived. The roaring wails rose from every nook and corner of the park.

The huge banners of three of the adjoining Housing Societies shook vigorously. People living in those flats rushed out on hearing the shrilling cries. They wondered whose anger had scared the people to death...waves of a violent tsunami were brewing in an ocean of pathos.

Hearing the through and through screams spearheaded by Cry Yoga Guru Swami Krandananda, flat residents trembled in disbelief. There was quite a massive crowd staring stupefied by the time the situation cooled down...two curious media persons with mike in hand, made their presence felt. Happy to notice a mike in their hand, Yoga Guru called for them.

Replying to the queries of the journalists Krandanandaji was able to emphasize the importance of Crying over Laughing. He explained, 'In life crying is a reality of man and society. Practice of this Yoga is more effective than best Yoga Combo. It is produced by agony of separation. The first poet too was a product of such agony. His pangs of sorrow created songs and his tears were a source of brilliant poetry. No where in history such a terrific poetry was ever created by laughter. Crying is so important that too much joy or excessive laughter brings tears in the eyes. So crying is our objective, crying is our life, crying is our God. For all the souls Crying is the path to reach God. If we ponder over the amount we cry in life, our perspective will broaden. If we elaborate upon them point by point, the seven oceans will fill to the brim. We will clear all doubts by discussing briefly only a few of those points, otherwise this place will get flooded. Many people cry for the looks they have got. They stand in front of the mirror, scrutinize themselves and blare at the injustice God has done while making their face. They never look at their inner beauty. Cry Yoga changes the looks and attention is diverted towards inner beauty. This is the magnificence of this Yoga.

Many persons cry over relationships. Some are not happy with their father, some with their son. I do not need to cry over the outcry of the rift between mother-in-law and daughter-in-law...you know all about it. Many times, our bosom friends is found hissing like snake of the sleeve. Then we shed silent tears!

Who has ever escaped crying in the office. For an easy escape 'Free Cry Practice' of Cry-Yoga is extremely effective. Nowadays both, love and onions are overpriced. They always make you cry...whether you cut them or not. How will laughter find a way to us. Cost of eating, chanting, housing, personal or public transport, dresses, costumes whether from China or antique always go higher and higher. Economic-Cry-Yoga Kriya will help cool it down. The prices will not fall but crying over them would definitely be less.

When you can't help crying at poor city sanitation or rising riches and glory of the neighbour, eyes shed copious tears while heart feels parched. Where to find an outlet for the feelings, where to find some breathing space? How to find a shirt better than that of the person next door? For all such pent-up frustrations our Guruji developed

'Tears of Malice-Yoga Kriya.' It is effective in neutralizing all jealousy, apprehension, fear and depression.

Are you considered as competent or brilliant as you are? Do you get fame and wealth you are worthy of? Most of you say 'no.' This is another reason for your eyes swelling with tears. To cool this mood 'Delusion-Diffuser Cry-Yoga-Kriya' will be practiced. You will not feel the pain as severely as you do now.

There are many other types of Cries, like making fakes, making duplicates, scathing reviews of TV serials, stupidity of children, noose of social media, untamed flow of floods, conversion of protectors to predators, fear hidden in fearless, generation gap and many more. They will not weaken your will power when we uplift you emotionally by practicing these morning sessions of 'Cry Yoga Exercise.' We guarantee that it will not let you cry the whole day.'

...Listening to the wise discourse of the learned Yoga Guru, all the journalists and assembled public heaved a 'Mass Sigh.' Under its spell, they forgot to clap in applause. Instead they had a Cry-Outburst and there was a mad rush to get to touch the feet of revered Guruji.

The Yoga Guru Swami Krandananda was moved by this utter devotion of the crowd. He had a fairly good idea of the truth behind heavenly bliss. Through mental Cry-Yoga within himself, he balanced himself. With an inner laugh, he got the Cry-Yoga-Camp inaugurated that very day.

□

8

Who Cares for the King?

'I don't give a damn, whoever is the King' has been the Indian mindset for ages. Every king with synonyms like ruler, emperor, monarch, sultan was pleased with the adorations sung in their glory and the cries for mercy made to them. Though the King treated them like slaves, they treated the King like their father. Now it's a different story but in that era how could a son stop respecting his father?

Before Bharat got her independence and autonomy, she was divided under the rule of not just ten twenty or hundred but five hundred sixty-five princely states or kingdoms. Thankfully we had the political leadership of Sardar Patel, the visionary 'Iron Man.' He meticulously brought all these different fragments under the rule and administration of Government of Bharat. The Jumbo-Purse of all the kings were withdrawn and money was made available for public utilisation. In lieu of it, Privy Purses were allotted to those kings. Over a period of time all the kingdoms got dissolved and slowly Privy Purse too was abolished.

Our independent country had the good fortune of the immaculate leadership of Sardar Patel for only three years and five months. After his demise the Princely States were back in place, albeit in a new form. The elected leaders were now the 'Kings.' The state became their personal property. It started flourishing, and bearing fruits. The bountiful produce was complemented by lavish Farm-House culture...very soon the Khadi, Cap and Khadi Kurta had a new meaning. From ordinary, they became distinctive. The dirty deeds of these aristocrats changed the black money for votes. The values of political system were martyred in the process.

Sandwiched between the pawns of note and vote, the demure voter was overwhelmed to be bestowed with the much-awaited Independence. On every 15th of August, he happily raised the slogan of Jaihind three times standing in front of Red Fort. He would cast his vote to elect his king and empty handed continue day dreaming for the time when the kingdoms would vanish. He kept waiting for those iron chains to give way in which those in power had tied down the lost memories of the Iron Man with the sinister intentions to demean his stature.

At last, it looked as though the wait was over. 597 feet tall statue of the Sardar was erected in the land of Mahatma... highest amongst all the statues in the world; higher than even the 'Statue of Liberty.' In principle it has been seen that even though it may take ages, but public is enthralled when the statue erected is of a personality close to their heart. That's why it is commonly seen that the self-erected statues of corrupt monarchs and dictators were dismantled all over the world and replaced by those who were respected by the commoners...they could be revered figures like Bhagat Singh, Subhash Chandra, Ambedkar, Azaad or Sardar Patel. It remains to be seen whether the tall statue worth 2063 crore rupees will just stand on a piece of land or would find as high a place in the heart of aristocrats.

□

9
The Truth of Now

The present matters the most in terms of time. The past affects our present and appreciation of the future is the compelling reality of present. Out of these three, present is the least of what we have. Whatever is less, is all the more valuable and a bit worrisome too.

The present time is full of dilemmas. At this time, we are facing both, natural and unnatural challenges. The life of city dwellers is specially messed up. Self-gratification is conspicuous everywhere and consumerism has made us egocentric.

School bags have become heavier but brilliance of education has faded away. Values have given way to price. What sustains its hold is what sells. Parameters of markets are supreme. Joint families are breaking up, relationships are cracking down, yoga is practiced to flaunt your assets.

Human beings have become like machines while machines have been humanised. Status of wed-lock has lost its dignity.

We have become Media-savvy. Media controls our day to day living, what we should eat, drink, how we should dress up, drape our attire. Even the soap and toothpaste to be used, how to keep our house clean, everything is decided by the media. We are no better than flies and mosquito trapped in the web of an illusion called fashion. Obsessive cut throat competition slashes our hands, we get irritated over why my shirt is less white than his!

Our teachings are now other way round. Earlier we were taught that sincerity is a supreme virtue. There always used to be a chapter that said 'Honesty is the best policy.' But now policies have been given new interpretations. Now honesty is a synonym of stupidity.

The position of seniors in the family is like that of a deserted orchard. Our houses have become like 'No man's land for them. If the house doesn't have a veranda, they have to find a place to sit.

Marshall McLuhan said, 'World is a Global Village.' No doubt we have become global in our living standards. Means of transportation and Telecom have made it a small world, but our 'Village' perspective has vanished. In a village anyone's daughter was like a daughter to the whole village but in the cities, our daughters are attacked by wolves every day. We have become close on Facebook but fail to recognize our neighbours when we meet them face to face. We don't get tired while posting likes on twitter but dislikes overpower us in our civil behaviour.

Our children are workshop material for America and Europe and get into the moulds of doctors, engineers and scientists to serve the foreign interests. We hesitate to honour our 'Bhartiya Identity while 'NRI' boosts our self-respect.

Being under debt was once considered sinful. Today it is counted as a blessing. No one needs to be told about the high status which Credit Cards bestow upon you since the time Plastic Money became a fad. These Credit Cards have become our Medals in their Gold and Platinum avatars. We have forgotten the real worth of words. A Degree has become synonymous with education. There is a mad rush for amassing as many degrees as possible. We feel happy to presume information to be the same as knowledge and have made Google our God. We believe in it. We try to change the system by changing the Governance. Actually, Governance changes but system remains as it was. We are only able to change colour of our caps which may be white, yellow or red but fail to change the system.

At present we are living in a myth. We assume that gathering more facilities will bring us more happiness and keep struggling towards them. As far as relationships are concerned, we find that our relationships are imposed upon us. We do not accept the reality. We constantly feel disappointed for what we wanted to happen but was not destined to happen. We want to have a brother who is like a friend, a friend who is like a brother. In the process we neither find a brother nor a friend.

We want to find a daughter in our daughter-in-law and mother in our mother-in-law. We just refuse to accept anything as it exists. In all our get togethers we are seen grumbling over our contacts and relationships.

We look for hotel like provisions at home and search for homely hotels. We love to have rustic decor in our city residences while we want to furnish village 'chaupal' in urban style. We have become so weird that we can't bear with the climatic conditions. In summer air conditioners chill us and we need drapes to sleep and in winters heat is turned so high that our homes have no breeze to cool us down.

We are living in the time of cultural collapse. All our TV Channels dedicated to Cultural awakening are twisting our cultural values.

Many judges of prestigious Reality TV shows, expose their own grave reality. The mannerism of disclosing high scores includes standing on desk or cheap whistling or obnoxious remarks. In this era of overwhelming cultural pollution, we do not find three hundred rupees for pizza or two hundred rupees for maggi or hundred rupees for popcorn to be unreasonable but a book is always considered to be expensive. We relish a two thousand rupees breakfast ordered on phone but our economy goes haywire while ordering a book online.

At this time, we are appreciating 'Bouquets' over 'Books.' We look for parking in place of parks. We are so eager to believe in marketing trends that we don't even observe how cheap these stunts are.

Today our 'True Economic Status' is our only truth. Our only goal is to amass wealth by hook or by crook. We have groomed ourselves build a society of middlemen. We find it respectful to become agents of those whom we should resist. We aim at those career prospects where corruption flourishes the most.

So far as merit is considered, we are aware that in our country a minimum qualification is needed to get a job of even fourth-class category but for those elected to govern us can even be illiterates.

If we take a look at our villages, our food growers, real 'Annadata' are so impoverished that they commit suicides out of frustration. We get to know from daily news that there is no injustice which has not been inflicted on backward classes. The local village judiciary in name of Khap Panchayat give death sentence to lovers that go against primitive social framework.

What time is this? We are passing away while the time is still. We are not relishing our pleasures; our pleasures are relishing upon us. Our deliberations are no more empowering. We are getting consumed by our own deliberations. Not our lust, we ourselves are becoming enfeebled.

In words of sage Bhartrihari—

Bhoga na bhukta vyamev bhukta,
Tapo na taptam vyamev tapta,
Kalo na yata vyamev yata
Trishna na jeerna, vyamev jeerna.

May Time be our saviour!

□

10
Running Train, Sparkling Rain

I am on train to Amritsar from Delhi. Reclining on seat number 3 of Swarn Jayanti Shatabdi I was engrossed in the newspaper. The view from the window attracted me from time to time. Light drizzle gave the sky light blue to dark grey hue. The train left about 20 minutes ago. A water bottle, butter milk and Newspaper has been provided for. The sky outside was still pleasant to look at but there was a stark difference in the ground reality... stretching far along the tracks, a sparkling 'grandeur' was teasing me...the decorative touch of plastic waste, glass pieces, paper, cardboard strewed carelessly redefined the parameters of beauty...and this was not all...sitting with their back exposed, some whimsical human beings, chanted the irony of Shrilal Shukla's 'Rag Darbari' while performing their morning chores...some were brave enough to look straight into the eyes of train travellers... after enlightening me about the much hyped success of government's cleanliness drive, my newspaper was lying tattered in shame and fear.

Rain drops are still trickling down...colours of the sky are as pleasing as before but the playful peacock in my heart is dead...suddenly rain drops are pouring venomous muck...I am trying to focus upon the gamut of drives making rounds around me...I draw the green curtains of the windows but as an educated citizen of fertile land of India, I feel disrobed.

□

11

Curious Renouncement of Principal Mathur

Principal Mathur submitted his resignation letter. The news spread like wild fire in the college campus that very day. During night it engulfed the entire university. He had occupied the chair just two months back and he has resigned. He was offered the chair for one year on the condition that if it didn't work out he would go back to his college. Otherwise after one year of deputation he would be made permanent as the College Principal. He had been selected for this post of Principal after he worked as a professor for thirty years in his previous college. He was not understood well because he was still new to the staff of this college. His morbid laughter flashed through everyone's mind. He laughed more than he spoke. No problem of the college could ever subdue his laughter. Even in staff meetings it was a universally accepted fact that he was an expert in drowning all conversations in his over-the-top laughter.

I had been his friend for long. Whenever I happened to catch up with him in his previous college, we together had tea and snacks. I was habituated to his rolling laughter-his posting as the principal of my college made him my boss and made me his one and only friend. As he took the charge officially, I was the first person to be entertained in his official cabin. Considering me to be his good old friend, he wanted me to help him out. Whenever I was not busy taking my own classes, I was supposed to be with him in his office and assist him in handling his administrative duties. He used to be in his office and as soon as I entered his office, he would welcome me with a gentle laughter and with a derisive laughter order the peon to get Samosa-Tea combo. I devoured Samosa and his cheerful belly laughter amused my ears. He would discuss official issues over etiquette laughter. During this whole process the hot savoury Samosa with fresh tea were my whole and sole focus of attention. At last Samosa with Tea became welcome entrants in Principal's office. I heard about his sudden renouncement from the office and went to his office as a friend-I was shocked that even after seeing me, there was not even a hint of laughter on his lips and area around. He held his head in both his hands. I asked him, 'Do you have a headache Dr. Sahib? I heard you just resigned from the post...what has made you do so? You were so happy here.'

He lifted his fingers away from his head. Glanced at me with gloom while rubbing his hands together-he could get a feel of my curiosity. He made a feeble attempt to become normal and got up from his chair. After closing the door instead of going back to his own seat, he came to sit on the chair next to me.

He held my hands and with deep anguish in his voice asked me, 'Are you permanent?' This was an extremely bizarre question. I answered, 'I am teaching for twenty-two years. Still, you are asking me this question?'

Gazing at the curious and startled expression on my face he said,' Then it is fine. I said, 'Please disclose what has happened Doctor Sahib. I am asking something else and you are answering something else!'

He took a deep breath and said, "Oh, when I entered college at nine this morning and after parking my car walked towards my office through the main lawn, I saw a dead cat under a tree. I told the worker who was watering the plants nearby, 'Get this cat removed from here.'

He said with folded hands that he was just a daily wage labourer. I should talk to the Head Gardner for this. I came to the office and called for the Head Gardner. He also came with folded hands and asked for my orders. I told him in my jovial style to remove the dead cat from under the mango tree. He heard me through both his ears and then replied in a restrained voice, 'Sir, I will just check!' I said 'What's there to check? Just remove the dead cat!' He shifted his shoulder drape from one side to the other and walked out.

He returned shortly thereafter and said, 'I have checked upon that Sir! This is not in my duty. Service book has no mention about it.' Before I could argue he vanished from there.

I was hot with irritation and insult. I called the S.O. and told him about the problem. He said unconcerned, 'Sir, what can I do about this?' I lost my cool and reminded him that he was a Section Officer. He should threaten the gardener and get the cat removed.

S.O. replied regretfully, 'Sir, there is A.O. over me. We work under his administrative orders. If you wish I can send him over to you.' A.O. came to me after about an hour. I repeated the entire story about getting the dead cat removed. I also informed him that the gardener is not accepting it as part of his duty.

A.O. said in a slow but confidence spruced voice that it was really not the duty of the gardener. Instead, the sanitation worker was responsible for it. Whenever there is such a mishap, it's managed by the sanitation worker.

I had lost my temper even before the sanitation worker entered my office. He listened to the problem and like the gardener talked about checking the Rule book. Now all hell broke loose. I retorted that I have already been told by the Administrative Officer that such matters have to be sorted by you. What was there to look in the Rule book?

The sanitation worker raised his brows and said, 'Sir when have I refused to carry out the job? Either me or someone from my department is going to remove it but I have to check the rate for doing so in the Rule book. I will just find it out and get back to you. I blocked his way and asked, 'Do you need to be paid extra for this? I know there is no such rule. You must be getting your full salary. 'He lifted his collar and said,' Sir, professors are paid extra money for checking answer sheets, in spite of getting their salary. They are paid extra for invigilation duty, extra TA-DA whenever they go out for governing body meetings. Why wouldn't we be paid extra? Just wait, I will get the rule book. You please see for yourself.'

I felt perplexed while I waited for the Rule book. S.O. and A.O. both came with the Rule book and the sanitation worker. Rule book clearly mentioned that extra money had to be paid for removing dead birds or animals from the campus.

Now I was Duty Bound and gave my authoritative order to get it removed before it started stinking.

All the three left and within five minutes the Sanitation worker was back with the Rule book. He showed me the page with the rates and said, Sir, there is a catch in it. 'I asked flabbergasted, 'What's it?'

He said,' It has mentioned rates for dead body of dog, crow, pigeon, small birds, mynah but not for cat! So, this job can't be carried out. It is against the rule.'

I got irritated and in that utter confusion raised my voice,' I will make sure that you get paid. Now you remove that dead cat. Take whatever you want. He said with a cunning smile, 'Sir, neither I nor you can tell the cat's rate. Even S.O. can't tell this. It can be decided only when the sanitation workers of this college hold a meeting with the Sanitation Workers Union of the University that the matter can be decided.'

I could see that my pride of being a College Principal was shattered to bits and pieces. My restraint gave way and I blasted,' Do you know you are answering back to the principal who holds the highest authority here. I can just chuck you out of your job.'

Hearing this that lower staff man got over me. In humiliating tone, he shouted at me, 'Principal sir, you can never chuck me out. I am a permanent employee. You are still temporary. A temporary employee has no authority to remove a permanent employee. On the other hand, permanent can definitely remove the temporary. "Saying this he banged the door and left my office. I repented that when I was happy at my own College, why the hell I came here? This is just the initial phase. Who knows what is in store? This matter was limited to the workers only. Then sometimes students would have raised their issues and sometimes lecturers would have become adamant...so I just submitted my resignation...I feel so relieved now..."

I came to an end of his sad story and stared at me with meaningful eyes.

I was stunned. I had no words and was left speechless.

To conclude: Mathur Sir has again started taking classes in his previous college...but his laughter is no longer the same as before!

□

12

Technical Avatar-ism

Just like Terrorism, Technical Avatar-ism is becoming a global phenomenon. In its new avatars Google is in the fast forward process of becoming God. It's a capsule of unlimited powers of the almighty. It is not only all knowing, omnipresent and omnipotent, it is easily available also. Its expanse is without boundaries. It is the ultimate decision maker. Its followers are it's true devotees...It takes one from the path of devotion to the path of knowledge. It can be accepted as the most knowledgeable avatar of our time.

There are some other avatars also which have replaced various erstwhile avatars. Vishwa Gram (Global village) has been replaced by Instagram. The 'face to face contacts have become Facebook contacts. There is remote to choose entertainment, tweet instead of personal conversation. Mobile phone has descended upon the earth and we no longer need to be mobile. It's like 'having the world in your pocket'! It is Brahma's Divine Aasan, Vishnu's Discus and Shiva's Damru. It is 'Trinity in Divine Soloism. '

The All-Knowing Mastermind called 'GPS-The Great,' knows all the ways to explore unknown destinations.

The historical Charvakism has reappeared as 'Credit Cardism.' Not just 'Ghee,' anyone can now procure whole of the Departmental store on Credit!

There are many more of these avatars but this much is sufficient to call it a day. Let's drop the falling flag of our Consciousness and take a Selfie of the Self-Within!

Amen!

□

13
Charisma of Nature

Religious sentiments gathered momentum as the Delhi Idols got decorated in the Regal Guest House at Napier Town, Jabalpur. The devotees anxious to have 'Devi Darshan' gazed in 'Trance Yoga Mode' whenever the Gods and Godesses of the hotel stepped out. Some of the Gods lost their cool thrice and irritated by their loathing devotion, were on the verge of demonstrating their Demonic abilities more than Divine to batter the sleazy emotions of the gazers! Thankfully, the dramatics did not survive beyond a verbal scene due to the 'Panchsheel Policy' of Sir Girish and Sudha Mam.

There was a lot of scope in Jabalpur for the students of Tourism. Lots of photos were shot. Many more notes were prepared here than in Bhopal. Besides Titu and Sunaina, several other couples had already arrived together by the time this 1800 km of the journey was covered. So photos had to rise in numbers. Robust Photo Sessions were in full swing. In the group of 46, there were 18 cameras and amongst these Prof. Suresh had an advanced version. Just by chance he was more thorough in working with camera angles than poetry or singing. He had been taking photographs of students during college

Programmes and trips. In a corner of the bathroom of his house he had a 'dark room' where he washed the negatives and clipped their positives on the strings tied in his balcony till, they dried and then carefully placed 'ready for dispatch' photographs in envelopes, which were labelled in accordance with a list of names along with the due amount as incurred in photo processing. Next, a record of collection of dues was made which at times took months because of the casual response of some of the difficult characters. It was obvious that whatever he earned out of it was well deserved for his skill and honesty, although he should not exhibit the same as a teacher!

It was an amazing scenic journey to aqua blue water gushing down the mighty waterfall. Rough and tough students like Sanjay Dewan gathered and imbibed a lot of information from Madan Mahal Fort, Fort of Rani Durgawati and Museum of Rani Durgawati. They even had several queries for the museum curator but the scholarly students found majestic marble rocks lying between the two brinks of River Narmada at Bhedaghat to be more interesting as well as scary. Girish Sir covered the shortcomings of his knowledge by being in constant touch with Sanjay Dewan throughout the Jabalpur journey. He publicly lectured and explained to each and every student, whatever information he gathered from Sanjay Dewan personally. Sanjay could sense that Sir was Dhritrashtra, but still giving him the Divine Vision was his moral duty.

Girish Sir stood solid like a rock by the side of swaggering Narmada, and talked to the students about the marble rocks of Bhedaghat 'Boys and girls (akin to brothers and sisters) at the moment, we are standing at Marble Rocks area on the bank of Narmada in Jabalpur District of India.

Golu muffled through his rounded-up lips, "Sir, by India, you mean India in Asia?" The question was in completion to the conversation but remained inaudible to the gracious ears of Sir, who was standing higher up. There was a series of subdued as well as loud laughter through those who heard it. This perturbed Sir Girish, but he continued, "River Narmada has carved this world-renowned, extremely beautiful Ghat stretched across eight kilometres by tossing aside the mountainous Marble Rocks with her powerful gushes."

This time Golu raised his voice like a powerful gush of Narmada and asked 'Sir is it eight or sixty?'

Girish Sir felt an abnormal uneasiness. His eyes filled with pitiful helplessness as he looked around for Sanjay Dewan. He could get a glimpse of him. Sanjay gave him the hint by raising his eight fingers but in confusion Sir could see only six and he informed,' Neither eight nor sixty, the ghat is six-kilometres!'

Jotting down the notes, Sunita quipped, "Sir but you just told eight!"

Sir said 'Take it as six only' and hurriedly shuffled down.

Not to say that he had no other option but to move down in such awkward situations.

The group boarded three boats and enjoyed the nature as they reached the eight-kilometre Ghat. The boatman had talked about to the depth of water from 'Elephant deep' to 'Camel Deep' and many more 'Deeps.' On reaching the midst of the lovely ghat the students pretended to be horrified as is the fashion on seeing Dracula movie.

In her trembling voice one of the girls asked the boatman 'Hi, no one ever drowned here?'

The query was unexpected but all on board awaited the answer.

'No ma'am, we have never seen in our lifetime. We have only heard that when Raj Kapoor was shooting here for his film 'Jis desh mein Ganga bahati hai' in which he himself and Padmini ma'am were acting, one of their lads fell in the water, but Ma Narmada tossed him up, next to Raj Kapoor!'

The talk about film shoot was more effective than oxygen in bringing thrill on the scared faces and visuals of the Vagabond Forever Raj Kapoor and Curvaceous Forever Padmini started floating in all eyes. There was a spurt of excitement. The entire sight looked pleasant and beautiful.

Rashmi gazed at Alok meaningfully as she asked 'Hey, which is the shooting spot of Raj Kapoor and Padmini? We will also take a photo there.'

RK Studio had overtaken the whole ambiance in which the tourists of all the three boats strolled around. The three boatmen pointed towards a spot of yellowish white shiny rocks where a pair of eagles were resting, one presumably was a male. Aiming at them the camera shutters swung into action and Ma Narmada swayed her waves in joy as she admired good looking boys and girls for their whole hearted dedication to their studies.

The 'Balancing Rock' known as 'Santulit Shila' was the last tourist destination in Jabalpur.

This is a mystical spot about which even Sanjay Dewan knew nothing. This world-famous spot is under the custody of Jabalpur Development Authority. A spherical rock is balanced over a huge sculpture for thousands of years. The tour group came over to have a look at it. Rajiv Sehgal read the information board while Sanjay Dewan jotted down the notes in his diary. Both tried to understand what it meant. Even after heavy brain storming, they could not comprehend much. Slowly the confusion spread to other students. Rajiv became their leader and announced a return of half the Trip Cost for the person who would interpret the information correctly. This provoked other students also to note down the information. Seated in every nook and corner they started the process of clearing up the confusion.

No one succeeded in understanding what it meant, even after one and a half hour and the matter made way to the teachers who were sitting under some trees at a little distance and discussing essential issues related to the tour. Girish Sir asked Rajiv to show his write up. He passed his notebook towards Sir in which he had written, 'A massive spherical rock balanced peculiarly on a huge rock at its Centre of Gravity. It was formed for geological reasons. There is no human involvement. It appears as though there was a prolonged period of wear and tear like processes after the formation of the rocky hill. This resulted in sticking together of soluble substances and separation of dispersible substances and the hard rock which balanced itself at its Centre of Gravity came into form. Its special feature is that it still exists in its original form due to its enormous size, weight, hardness and exact alignment of Centre of Gravity.

Girish Sir went through it twice and handed it over to Sudhi Ma'am saying 'I don't understand it but the word 'form' came three times...it was written as 'from' which is a great example of a word mis-spelt. Sudhi Ma'am went through it several times and said 'I can understand the meaning of the words but cannot make out what it is trying to communicate. Let's ask Prof. Suresh. He is a Hindi Poet. Maybe he can explain this brief. '

Prof. Suresh also went through it with utmost attention but the meaning was twisted like a dog's tail. It had decided to remain twisted, so it did. Expressing his inability, he said 'I cannot follow every message completely, just because I write poetry. I do know a perfect method to interpret this type of Hindi.'

'What's it?' Rajiv Sehgal raised his voice.

'Do tell us, please 'Sudhi Ma'am asked endearingly.

'Let me explain, whenever this kind of Hindi is written on the door of an office, there is always another door with an English version also. By reading it, you can understand the Hindi write up. Rajiv, check near the 'Balancing Rock 'for a brief in English. Note it down and bring it to me. Even if you don't write it, you will definitely understand in English. Then you can explain it to us.'

Rajiv Sehgal, the leader and Deputy Kamal Rustogi rushed straight in search of the English Board. They returned in twenty minutes with the information that they found no information in English. This disheartened Girish.

'Sir-said, No, the information in English is not available and we can't understand it in Hindi.'

We could have interpreted he, it if it was in English and still people are so much averse to English.'

Even though the meaning was not clear, all cameras were fully operational to shoot the rock from all possible angles, Right, Left, Top, Bottom.

In the summary session Golu kept wondering in a serious philosophical mood. His thoughtfulness and his walk slowed down. While returning he stayed back as the group moved ahead. He rushed towards the 'Balancing Rock,' observed it carefully, analysed and then found a seven to eight kilo piece of flat bottom stone and placed it on top of the smaller rock lying over the lower gigantic rock...now a rock was visible over a rock, with another rock above it.

He ran back to his group and mixed up in them like a fake coin gets mixed in real ones. No one was aware about what he was up to and his secret mission was accomplished the next day.

Bhopal to Bombay train was awaited. An engine was supposed to connect to bogie number 2203 stationed in the yard and move it to the right track for alignment with the train when it arrived.

Most of the students were inside the bogie. Girish Sir, Rajiv Sehgal and Kamal Rustogi were standing alert on the platform. Girish Sir was habituated to chewing upon daily newspaper with a cup of tea. He got tea and Newspaper through Kamal. After a Cleanliness Drive of dusting the railway bench to some extent he made himself comfortable on it to sip his cup of tea and chew the newspaper. It was a local paper, printed in dark ink. What the hell! He got alarmed at a picture published on its front page. Putting off his cup on the bench, he secured the paper with both his hand and immersed himself in it. The picture shown was of the Balancing Rock they had looked at and analysed a day before. What amazed and confused Girish Sir was that another rock was visible over the huge base rock. He started going through the details provided alongside. It said, 'World famous Balancing Rock at Jabalpur added to the surprise element of visitors last evening. Miraculous Nature revealed a Baby Rock glued above the smaller rock balanced for thousands of years over the Big Rock at the base. The City Authorities will get Geo Scientists to investigate the phenomenon.

The Triple Rock picture was labelled 'Miraculous Nature: Birthing Rock.' Kamal told Girish Sir there was a massive crowd at the railway stall to buy this newspaper and that's how he got late.

Golu, The God who was behind all this magic, relaxed in Vishnu Pose in bogie No. 2203, unaware of his Divine Powers.

□

14
A Wash for Gandhiji

As soon as October comes, Gandhiji' s name and fame is made to rise and shine. Wherever any big or small statue of Gandiji is found installed, it is adorned with garlands. On 2nd of October Gandhiji is the topic of discussion just like the Farmer's issues, Poverty and Scams are in the rest of the year.

Last year, two days before 2nd of October, Bela Pur Municipal Corporation got an order from the City Chief to wash up Mahatma Gandhi's statue installed in the city. The Municipality In charge sent a humble reply that the location of the statue is no longer under them. It was under Greater Bela Pur Municipal Corporation. So, the order should be issued to them.

The City Chief addressed the order to Greater Bela Pur Municipal Corporation but again a similar reply was received. They said that the area was once under them but they had no knowledge about which authority it was under now!

The matter became so controversial that the statue could not be cleaned up. Gandhiji's devotees had organised a Charkha Programme and Bhajan Singing in front of the statue on the morning of 2nd of October. Local

Political Leaders were supposed to deliver lectures there after that.

Looking at the statue covered with pigeon droppings and dust the lower staff leaders started preparing to raise a protest campaign. In the unruly aftermath, the song, 'Vaishnavjan...' got interrupted mid-way. The devotees soon turned into goons.

Soon the campaign turned ugly. After all it was a matter of respecting The Father of the Nation. Vehicles were set ablaze, police had to resort to lathi charge and the city had to be shut down. The patriotic political leaders celebrated the success of the event by indulging heavily in drinks in a drink party and in an inebriated state, they slept like dogs!

2nd of October is again coming; close preparations are in full swing...Gandhiji's statue has still not been washed up.

□

15
The Divine Herald

Indian culture is dominated by deities. Indian devotional ethos is based on Deity-Worship. It is believed that we have Thirty-three 'Koti' deities. According to some wise men the number of deities is only six hundred and sixty. The count of 'Koti' means Crore which is equivalent of ten million. But some take 'Koti' to mean Twenty. Some philosophers consider, 'Koti' as variety. So according to them deities are of Thirty-three types.

If we intend to contemplate upon deities, we should understand their qualities. Our fore-fathers have revealed to us that their most prominent quality is that 'Deities never let their feet touch the ground.' Their various other qualities are that they never blink their eyes, they never sweat, they remain young forever, they never fall ill. They are always in company of beautiful 'Apsaras,' they don't cast a shadow, and relish sipping Som-rasa 'Nectar of Delight.' Their body never gets mucky, the flower garland around their neck never withers, they shower fresh flowers on those they are happy with etc. etc.!

The deities must be having some other qualities also, but these are what they are popular for. If we want to analyse critically, we will have to look at their numbers first of all. According to their qualities the most renowned deities are Five hundred and fifty-two. They are offered prayers in a heavenly circular edifice. They usually refrain from putting their feet on the ground. They are provided with high-end vehicles for their movement. They carry them for their journey on the earth as well as across the sky with air-planes! These deities appear to blink their eyes. But these are just outer eyelashes. They never blink their inner eyelashes because theoretically their Deity Status can be withdrawn as soon as they do so. They stay in well controlled environment and need not do any physical labour. That's why they don't sweat. Their lifestyle is such that they are always full of youthful energy which keeps them ever young. Sometimes they are seen hovering over 'Apsaras' and sometimes 'Apsaras' are seen hovering over them.

Deities are self-sufficient and people never get to see even their shadow. They whole heartedly indulge in consuming 'Soma-rasa,' The Nectar of Delight from Monday to Sunday. Their luxurious and lavish style removes all muck from their body and deposits it on their mind. So their body is never soiled. Deities are offered fresh flower garlands around their neck all the time, so they never lose their freshness. Deities are usually pampered at Honourable Missions like Inauguration functions, Laying of Foundation Stones, presiding over various functions or occupying the chair of Chief Guest. At such places their words of grace shower flowers on those who flatter them just like they did on them!

So it can be concluded that the qualities of Deities as seen in common people, are factually proven.

Thus Ends the Divine Herald Narration.

□

16
Superman

We have been reading and listening to the tales of Ramayan and Mahabharata since our childhood.

In Ramayana we are impressed by the powers of Hanuman while the might of Bheem in Mahabharata leaves us spellbound.

As children we wondered how Hanuman could overpower more than twenty monsters on his own. The enemy set his tail ablaze and he reduced the whole of Golden Lanka to ashes. Hanuman also had amazing power to fly across the ocean.

Superman Bheem was as robust as hundred elephants. He was identical to Hanuman, in ruthless thrashing of his enemy. We got to learn about his son Ghatotkach. At the time of his heavenly departure after death, he became such a huge hulk that millions of enemy soldiers got crumbled under his weight.

As we grew up, all this appeared fictitious to us. But when we started seeing Hindi and other language movies, we realised that our filmy heroes were much more powerful than those gutsy brave-hearts.

An ordinary looking hero enters the den of crooks, all by himself. With effortless ease he bashes up more than twenty herculean brutes. Even if the savage beasts are in possession of knives, hacks or pistols, the weapon less hero either sabotage their weapons or is shrewd enough to kill them with their own weapons.

If the movie hero is a police officer, he proceeds alone on his motorbike or Jeep to meet the challenge. Without any other policeman to assist him, he smashes the hideout of Don and brings laurels for police force.

In case the hero is a dacoit, thief, pick pocket or a goon, he still moves on his own in a wayward car or a jeep which always happens to be open for him. Whether it has a key or not doesn't really matter. Its fuel tank is always full much beyond its capacity! His car flies past all policemen chasing him. They all are left miles behind in their pursuit. He trashes their jeeps and absconds. That's when we feel amused at the deplorable state of police and don't mind applauding the gangster.

Even if our hero is a school dropout, he has all the knowledge about medical science, engineering and every possible field of education. He can easily fly a plane or diffuse a time bomb. He needs no degree, training or experience. He acquires everything before he is born.

Our hero can loot or murder anyone, but he is always such a decent guy that the daughter of a Police Commissioner, Minister, Chief Justice or Industrialist is head over heels in love with him and is willing to go to his home and family for his sake...our hero can do everything that Hanuman or Bheem could do, but besides the show of strength, there are many more things that he can do which even Hanuman and Bheem were not able do! He can sing melodious songs in perfect rhythm. He even composes the lyrics while he sings. He can dance in any style and never misses a beat. He is always impeccably dressed in designer clothes, even if he lives with his old mother in a shanty. Now just imagine how Hanuman or Bheem could be so versatile?

A frail looking hero, typically from South Indian movies throws five-six scoundrels five-six feet high in the air with the single blow of his fist and then gives a cool smile to the ruffians running towards him with hatchet in their hands, we are rest assured that he will welcome them with a mighty blow and will escape without a scratch!

Quite often the hero proves to be a generous social reformer for his enemies. He comes in a wagon or a huge vehicle. After beating them all black and blue, he loads them in his vehicle and carries them to a hospital... whenever the hero performs such out of the world daring feats, the spectators clap in jubilation. They hardly know that in the Auditorium or wherever the show is running, Hanuman and Bheem standing in some corner, in their shrunken or invisible avatars (akin to Mr. India) are watching it all with tearful eyes and folded hands.

□

17
Third Time Visit to In-laws

How sweet are the reminiscences of the days when I visited my in-laws for the first time after getting married. The gala reception I got would not have been given to even a Nation's Head after winning elections. Two of my younger sisters-in-law waited at the gates with bouquets in their hands...everything was so royal! For my smallest request for anything, two to three persons would run around. Full of affection, my mother-in-law caressed my head so fervently that I got worrisome for my hair falling away.

On my second visit only one SIL was at the gate, sans any token of welcome. When I asked for something, it was brought by the maid. MIL accepted my greeting from a distance and simply raised her hands to bless me from a distance.

Friends, when I visited my in-laws for the third time, I was already married for six months...the entrance looked desolate and deserted. One of the SIL was at college and the other one was busy with a next-door friend. For some strange reason my throat felt dry within ten minutes of reaching there...my wife went inside and got absorbed in sorting her childhood photos and books stacked in the cupboard of her pre-marriage era. My FIL was in full relaxation mood in the comforts of his bed. Having been thirsty for quite some time, I looked around for some help. Till then, no one had given me any attention, whatsoever! When thirsty, the only support is one's wife. I called her on mobile and told her about my condition. Her reply was hopelessly demeaning. She said, 'Prof. in the room adjacent to where you are, is a table with some glasses. Wash one of the glasses and pour some water from the fridge. 'I tried to say something but she felt I was being crude. She replied, 'Now will you stop bothering me and help yourself!'

I made a humble request, 'Please send the maid, she will get me a glass of water. 'This was the last straw. She reacted fiercely, 'I have come to understand in the last 4 months that you are thirsty just because you expect the young maid to get water for you...I can see through you, Professor!'

First, I was addressed as 'Darling.' It was all refined sugary in the first month, then in the second month it became raw jaggery. Third month was jaggery with a handful of salt and now in the fourth month everything had turned sour...now in my in-laws house I am addressed by the title used by my FIL...let's leave this matter here for the time being...and get back on the issue of my 'thirst.' Even thirsty crow who brought pebbles in his beak would not have been so thirsty. On top of that I was being accused of being 'thirsty' because I was looking for an excuse to call the maid. I felt like banging my head against a wall, but the wall was a little too far...having no other option I called upon the Columbus inside me! I located the glass, filled it with water and quenched my thirst. This way I personified the proverb 'To drink water and then curse'! I was the SIL-Damaad for whom no one cared. The people who rushed on my one call, were nowhere to be seen.

To take care of my loneliness, my FIL made an entry. He was fresh after completing his peaceful nap.

He ask, How are you doing, Professor?' I bent to touch his feet in reverence and heard his Blessings 'Truth alone wins'!

I solemnly replied, 'Babuji, I am not too well!'

'Why so? What happened?'

'I am the 'Damaad' of your house, but the prestige of 'Damaad' was too short lived. I am here, in this room for more than an hour and no one has paid any attention to me. Even this glass of water...'

Cutting off sentence, FIL replied with an annoying laughter, 'Professor, do you know when one becomes 'Damaad' his 'Daam' i.e., value drops by half. The grandeur is just a momentary illusion. After that it is...Hahaha....' He had a bout of hysterical laughter and I got disoriented.

After a gap he said, 'Professor, we have also passed through this phase. The only difference is that now it gets dark pretty soon. In our time the moonlight shone much longer. When you will become a FIL you will also understand this and that guy who will be your Damaad...!'

I now felt amazed listening to his words. Just then like God Vishnu appeared at the pathetic call of Puranic Gajendra, Babuji's neighbour Vishnu appeared without my calling him...his arrival was a relief to me, the Gajendra.

That day meals were served in a huge platter but there was neither any paneer nor any kofta curry. I felt getting baked when tasteless gourds and watery chana dal was served. Oh, what an anti-climax! When I had visited the first time, I was given a variety of options from the menu...and how I was pampered and made to cherish all the savoury dishes...today I was somehow gulping whatever was available...Babuji was enjoying every bite. All others were somewhere out of sight...I was able to understand what it means to be like an 'unwanted guest.'

Friends, I swear by God, that day I felt so frustrated with my own self. Why the hell did I take leave from college on the command of my wife. In College I know how to trick my students. I would tactfully manage to be in the staff room at that time and enjoy political discussion on international issues over a cup of coffee. I could have avoided this poisonous dose of Home Planners Generosity. Even a sip of water was hard to have, all laughter was lost and food had played havoc with my poor tongue.

I was suffering from an identity crisis. I sent an SMS to my wife. 'Please come soon, let's go home. If you wish to stay on, please do so. I have to leave to prepare notes for the MA students. You may come whenever you wish to. But I won't be coming to pick you up.'

My wife came rushing like the rising price index... 'Oh, I understand everything. Here there is no one close to your heart. There you will just loiter around in the neighbourhood instead of making any notes...I know it all' she kept mumbling!

It was my in-law's house. There was no scope for me to make any excuses. My FIL had already passed his judgement...my value had fallen from half to one fourth by now...Alas, from one whole to half and now to one fourth...???

Only six months had passed. Now I'm quite accustomed to what happens after that. The third trip was an educational expedition. Those of you who are married, must be knowing...No?

□

18
Cool Cat Devotion

It was a Sunday. While having my morning stroll, I happened to reach Aunt Toshi's house. I had just been transferred to the city. I pressed the call-bell. I could neither hear anyone reply nor bark in response. I pushed the door gently and it opened. I found myself inside the house.

I was bemused by what I saw inside. A film song could be heard loud and clear—*'Billo rani kaho to apni jaan de doon.'* Aunty was whole heartedly engrossed in singing alone the song and dancing on the music. I wondered how could my rather old aunt enjoy such an item song?

Unwittingly, Aunty opened her eyes and gazed at me. She put off the music and blessed me as I greeted her. I lifted my curious face and asked, 'Why were you dancing around on this film song so early in the morning?'

'Oh Dear! Which Film song? Nay, this is a lovely devotional song. This is how my morning prayers begin. It takes me to the era of Dwapar and I wish to keep dancing like a Gopi with Krishna. This song is actually Vrindavan Raas...!'

'Devotional song?' I said reluctantly. 'How do you call it a devotional song? *Billo rani kaho to...???* Uff Aunty, you are so impossible...!'

She raised her pitch bad and said, 'Dear, have you lost your mind? What do you understand from this song? The song has such deep devotion and divine love...!'

'Aunty, what are you saying? *Billo rani kaho to...???* I asked disgusted.

Aunty said, 'Girls with beautiful cat like eyes are called—*Billo!!!* You won't understand...in this song Krishna is requesting Radha to cast away her anger at him and reconcile with him. He is even willing to sacrifice his life for her love. My dear, you should see the devotion expressed in this song...!'

I realised that it would be impolite to mention anything about *'Billo rani'* again. I made myself comfortable on the sofa and said, 'I see, I had got it wrong. Aunty you must be having many more devotional songs like these!'

She said elated, 'Of course, there are several of them. I listen to all of them and then meditate upon them...one of them comes time and again on TV...*'Om Shanti Om, Shanti Shanti Om'*...shall I play it?'

'Oh no, let it be!' I was now getting interested in Aunt's favourite prayer songs. The way she elucidated the depth of such songs gave me an eerie pleasure. I asked her, 'Which other songs do you find devotional?'

She said, "When you were still a child, a song by Swami Devanand became extremely popular...Hare Rama-Hare Krishna". I was a young girl at that time but still relished such prayers. Then another one became popular. You must be in 7th or 8th class at that time...*'Jai Jai Shiv Shankar, kanta lage na kankar, ki pyala tere naam ka piya...saun rabb di!'*

I blurted out, 'Yes, the one by Swami Rajesh Khannaji Maharaj!'

'Perhaps, I don't remember too clearly now...but it was definitely by some Mahamandeleshwarji.'

Then when you reached higher classes, a song of Mira was sung by Amitabh Bachhan *"Hmmmm, ke pag ghunghroo bandh Mira nachi thi...*rendered beautifully. Mirabai was unmatched, so is Amitabhji, how divine...!

I could no longer restrain myself and said with a crooked smile, 'Yeah Aunty, I have got the next line, *'Vo teer bhala kis kaam ka hai, jo teer nishane se chuke chuke re...'*

This delighted my aunt, 'Yes yes, that was the arrow of Ramchandraji, how could it miss the target? Rama had prayed to Shiva to gain victory over Ravana, that's why his arrow hit the target...Dear, you must study Mahabharata and Ramayana. This improves your religious knowledge. Listen to such soulful devotional songs every day in the morning. It will make you cheerful and purify your heart...'

I was really impressed by her words. I was trying to assess the height her perceptions had achieved. It was then that Uncle returned from his morning walk. I touched his feet and got his blessings. He said, 'It's good you have come so early in the morning. Now we will have a cup of tea but first let me play my favourite devotional song...' He started the music player and I could hear the famous *kawwali* of that era *'Ye ishk ishk hai ishk ishk...'* I was flabbergasted when I saw my uncle dance at it singing *'Krishna Krishna Krishna Krishna!'*

□

19

Thinking about Poor—A Flattering Trap

'Who is poor?' He asked a simple and straightforward question.

Gurudev felt uneasy at the query of the Crown Prince. It was expected that he would not go wrong with his answer. It was not a tough question but he felt it difficult to answer. Still, he tried and said, 'Poor is the one who doesn't have a house of his own or bread to eat or clothing to wear.'

The young prince went into deep introspection. He returned after a short break and asked, 'Gurudev, people living in the Capital don't have their own houses. Most of them live in rented accommodation.'

'We all know that the house rentals shoot up every now and then. If one can pay such high rates, how can he be poor? All the restaurants, food courts and kiosks have heavy rush...it's difficult to find a place to sit. But hardly anyone can be seen eating bread. Everyone is seen enjoying chowmin, dosa, bhatoora, pizza, burger, puri, sandwich etc. One who can spend so much for such dishes, how can he be poor? If you excuse me Gurudev, the third point is that even you are not appropriately dressed. You have draped just a saffron piece of cloth.'

'The other day you take to Haridwar for Kumbh festival...the swami and saints were half naked. Naga Sadhu actually wore nothing at all. They were having a majestic parade with pomp and show. Some were even on decorated elephants. They all have huge hermitage. They can be considered poor...they behaved like royal dignitaries.'

Gurudev hesitated for a moment. He was groping for words. He himself was semi dressed. He came every day to give him Yoga training and answering his queries. He had been gifted a posh car by the queen mother for this purpose.

Though clueless he said, 'O Crown Prince, poor is the person who remains unheard. He is not able to speak out his mind.'

I have read in the newspaper and heard on TV channels that Judges are not being, heard. The teachers and professors are not being heard. Traders, engineers and doctors have resorted to strike because they are not being heard. Are they poor?'

Gurudev felt miserable. He had failed to give a convincing answer to the prince who was less than half his age. He tried to frame his words and when enlightened said, 'One who is jobless is poor!'

The young king stood up. His embellished robes were glittering. He laughed and asked, 'Gurudev are we poor? We don't have a job. Many of our jobless friends move around in BMW or Parado...some in Ferrari. Can they or those like them be called poor? I don't think so!!!' He was rolling in laughter.

Gurudev found the conversation getting unbearable.

A song hinted him, 'Run Milkha, run'-but he was not lucky enough to run anywhere.

Prince mocked at him, 'Gurudev, you can't even tell who is poor? Is this all your knowledge and wisdom? Just think a little harder. You may do some Kapalbhati!'

Gurudev was hit gravely by these words. He kept stroking the long locks of hair growing on his head. The prince was sunk in the fluffy coach but his eyeballs were following his fingertips. He was thoroughly amused. Today he had trampled his sky rocketing ego.

Gurudev came out with another statement, 'Look prince, poor is the one who has no bank balance and hold no cash.'

The prince thought over and put a final query, 'Gurudev, in our Capital there are several people with plenty of black money. They don't keep any bank account.'

'Many a time they have no money in hand, not even something to hold money. You mean they are poor?'

Gurudev was dumbfounded. He felt his wisdom and practice was good for nothing. Still, he tried and said, 'O prince, poor is the person in whom no one has any faith.'

The prince got furious. He threw hard hitting words on Gurudev and said, 'Gurudev, right in the centre of this Capital, there is huge Circular structure covered with a lot of greenery. No one believes in the people who enter it. City dwellers don't believe in their administrators and legislators. Are the inhabitants of that Circular building all poor?

'Gurudev, you are able to give sermons to the whole world but when you come to our residence it seems you have just been herded here. You are just beating about the bush. I don't like it. Now tell why hard work is done by poor people? I will not rest till you answer this...cone on think!'

This question gave Gurudev something he was looking for. It showed him the way to come out his inferiority complex. Thinking a little deeper rewarded him with some brilliant pearls of wisdom. He said, 'O prince, the poor person is a labourer. He gets paid on daily or hourly basis...'

Stopping him midway, prince said, 'Daily or hourly basis? Isn't it same as wages? The masterji who comes to teach me Hindi, is paid by mother queen on hourly basis. He is not paid for the days he absents himself. He doesn't look poor. He comes by his own car. He has a flat in the Capital and another one in Mussouri. Is he poor? So many private companies pay on hourly basis. Our new generation is not interested in Government jobs. The youth want to work in private companies which pay on hourly basis. Companies send them for on-shore assignments at its own expenses. No, this won't do, give me another answer!'

'Yes, yes, that's what I was coming to. 'Gurudev replied cleverly. 'Poor is possibly he, who sells milk, gives a haircut, washes our clothes, repairs shoes, cleans up the filth...etc.' and he heaved a sigh of relief. He was confident that now the prince will be satisfied with the answer. There was still a fear that prince who had the knack of skinning every detail, and had quashed his explanations on several earlier occasions, was quite unpredictable and may have still something up his sleeve.

His apprehension was not unfounded. The prince picked up the semi stitched coat of Gurudev's answer and tore it to pieces.

He said 'How can you say that? Don't you know that the milkman who supplies us milk cones in his own jeep. He left his army job to sell milk to big houses-he soon became a member of that circular building and even got elected as a minister. This proves you wrong.

'Now the barbers...my father takes me to a five-star hotel for his own and my hair cut. First the barber in the salon cuts our hair and then we have breakfast in the hotel restaurant. Either we go to them or the hair dresser from the salon comes to our Bungalow. Their salon has branches not only in the Capital, but several other cities also-and you say barbers are poor!'

'The washer man also has the same history. Our ancestors' clothes were sent to foreign countries to be cleaned. Then the appropriate facility was not available in our country. Now a days every local market has one such laundry shop. Everyone uses their services. How can you know anything about how much they earn, you don't have much to wear any way...you just drape whatever you have!'

'Now do you need to be told about the shoe makers? Forget about our own companies, even foreign brands earn a heavy amount by doing shoe repair job for us. This also cannot be defined as poor.'

'Cleaning up the filth is an industry now. It is easily accessible, on contract. They take up the responsibility fir your residence, complex or institution and would give cleaning and maintenance services for a monthly or annual amount. Gurudev, the workers with these companies arrive with ultra-modern sweeping and cleaning gadgets... Gurudev if you still have anything to add, please do, by all means. But please let me know who is poor???'

Gurudev was in doldrums. His lips had frozen and he was all ears. He knew that the prince could not differentiate between discussion and futile arguments. He knew that though the prince was incapable of telling truth and facts from facts and illusion he was capable enough to reduce the great person like Gurudev to an insignificant shortie because trapped in the system, such people can't let go of the agonising flattery mantra.

As soon as the prince gave rest to his voice, Gurudev closed his ears. His body had become soul which was dying steadily-even then a question kept haunting him, 'Who is poor?'

In that moment he felt himself to be squarely poor!

□

20
Fuse of Confusion

I was preparing myself for Independence Day celebrations when I heard someone ask, 'Son, can you tell me the difference between India and Bharat? I keep hearing about the two now and then. Are they both not the same?'

An elderly neighbour Shantilal, whom I addressed as Chachaji asked keenly. I replied, 'Chachaji, when people follow western etiquette in eating food and communicating, it is called India and when people follow native mannerism, it is called Bharat.

'My dear, western etiquette is observed mainly in England. Then would it be considered India?'

I felt dazed. I tried to explain, 'Leave aside England. Within our country 'India' is used for those people who speak English, wear western style attire, whose children study in English schools and 'Bharat' for those who wear our traditional dresses like kurta-pyjama, saree, dhoti, headgear...'

I felt I had answered what he sought and I would get a pat on my back but he said in an authoritative voice, 'I don't agree. Three months back I went to my Haryana village. There was a Birthday Party for the grandson of

Sarpanch. All guests were dressed in local costumes. They were even talking in their local slang but the birthday cake to be cut was of western style. It was decorated with little candles and when children started blowing them off, all villagers loudly sang 'Happy Birthday to you...'! Now was this India or Bharat?'

Now my head was spinning. I said, 'Chachaji, it's a matter of deep concern...!'

'How deep? As deep as a trench or a well?'

Now what could I say. I could actually visualise Bharat vs. India as a trench vs. a well, wherever I will fall, I was sure to injure myself. I hesitated before I said, 'It's just a matter of your perspective. Those whose perspective is for the Nation, are called Bharat and those whose perspective is for western culture and English culture are called India.

They mean one and the same, but are...'

'...but what? Tell me Dear, those who teach Sitar, Tabla or Yoga to people in England and replace their perspective with our perspective, do they make them 'Indian'? Those who go from here to western countries and give lectures in English, mix up with people of England, what are they... Indian, Bhartiya or English men?'

Now the matter had gone over my head. I retorted, 'Chachaji, perspective means the difference in the mindset of those who go to Public Schools and those who go to other schools..., I can't make you understand, you try to make out the difference yourself! I am so short of time...I have still got to go and get new Tricolour Flag...'

'My Dear you are a College Professor and teach so many things there but it seems you are not clear yourself. You are just confusing me for the past half an hour.

Actually, you yourself are confused. I had an impression that you are highly intelligent but...'

I was forced to keep my mouth shut. I felt that I am actually confused. Rather whole of the Nation is confused in the matter of Bharat and India. I heard Chachaji say, 'Dear, neither am I ignorant nor confused. I was just testing your mental level. Now Professor, listen to me. The solution is just too simple. You don't have to solve the dilemma between Bharat and India. All of us have to realize that more important than Bharat or India is Hindustan. Look for it and have a sense of belonging to it. Then our Independence Day celebration will become meaningful!'

In my delusion I felt that the fuse of my confusion was getting re-joined...

□

21
Rally Power

We have a special system of measuring Show of Power. It is called 'Rally.' According to the Great Hindi Dictionary, the word 'Rall' means a planetary configuration, group or cluster. Putting a 'y' as a suffix means-a collection of planets, groups or clusters. Rally incorporates all the three interwoven in each other.

Rally is an interplay of a planetary phenomenon. It can change the future happenings in the fortunes of a leader. Another meaning of this term is associated with money. It gets transferred in pouches. Rally and these pouches are hand and glove with each other. In rallies such pouches are offered to the leaders on the pretext of public donations. Actually they are an offering by those who have their own axe to grind. Public is a party merely by default.

The other meaning of rally is 'group.' This term comes to life according to the religion, caste, state inhabited, lingo, business etc. These rallies are held according to this formula, by these different groups, for these different groups and are made up of these different groups. The root base for this to work is 'Divide and Rule!'

The third point of rally is 'cluster.'

Cluster means 'herd of speechless animals like sheep, goat, cows and buffaloes. This is truly symbolic because people in this category are actually 'herded' together in the rallies.

Like cows and buffaloes, they too are made use of... they are merely clusters and are inconsequential. They can be fleeced or skinned as required. They are meant to fulfil the ambitions of such rallies...the 'Fifth Pillar' also needs the rallies as their fodder. If there are no rallies, Media Houses will flop, TRP will nosedive.

Without rallies, the Nationalists will get suffocated. Rally is their Birth right and it is the solemn duty of common public to come forward for it.

Amen!

□

22
Disillusioned

A bitch was smitten by human beings. She craved to be a woman and wished to get rid of being hounded by dogs. She performed tough penance. God appeared before her and allowed her to ask for a boon. The bitch said, 'O God, may I retain my dog-instinct but get converted to human species!' God said 'May it be so!' and disappeared.

The bitch became an enchanting lady and got allured by men. Soon she again started with a penance. God appeared and this time she prayed to be a bitch again.

'But why?' God was curious to know.

'Now I know God, that human beings are far ahead of dogs in their dog like behaviour!'

□

23
Towards Award Evaluation

There is a peculiar uneasiness when anyone misses out on an expected award. Research analysts have found that this agony can be more deeper than that of a marriageable girl who fails to find a suitable match or when an ardent social worker fails to get an election ticket. Now, what do these analysts say about those who keep getting awards over and over again?

In their opinion, recipients of recurrent awards become either like animals who have tasted human blood or like such politicians who have been Ministers for ages. The anguish of such award winners is quite similar to blood thirsty brutes who do not get human blood or outdated politicians who fail to secure the post of a Minister. The condition of a wild animal who has tasted human blood, a politician itching to be a Minister and one who is sick of receiving repeated awards is religiously similar.

The literary scholars who fail to get an Award over a span of a month, get pangs of disappointment in their heart and feel disgusted within. If a whole year remains barren, their physical and mental misery cannot be measured in words.

If we try to categorize the Awards, the best are those which provide some cash too. The amount received is reciprocated in the amount of arrogance exhibited. The ego of the recipient gets inflated according to the inflation of the 'Packet' of envelope.

In one class of Mega Award Function, the awardee is honoured with a 'Shawl' as a token of respect. A 'Shawl' is a symbol of high esteem. Receiving an Award brings in 'chill.' The 'Shawl' helps the writer beat the chill and prepares him to face another Season of Chill!

The 'Shawl' literally glorifies the literary world. The literary genius keeps it in his safe custody along with its tag and cover. Then it can be gifted away. On the auspicious occasion of someone's Birthday, Wedding Anniversary, Housewarming Party, A New-born's Arrival, the 'Shawl' is presented with full gusto to the worthy recipient and the presenter exalts himself. While draping 'Shawl,' utmost attention is given to the proper visibility of the tag. It should be clear that the 'Shawl' has been just purchased from the market. It's noteworthy that at any such occasion a literary giant hardly ever presents a 'Shawl 'to another literary giant...the reason might be hidden from you but not from them.

There are some Esteemed Award Ceremonies where only Appreciation Certificates are issued, with or without any honour. Such 'Appreciation Certificates' are also of different categories. Some of them are like a bridegroom's 'Sehra' whence the relationships are the same as before but somewhat redefined. The adjectives to honour the recipient are traditional except that the names are changed. The matter in the middle part remains untouched. Only the title on the top and the names of those who are giving away the awards are changed. The Awardee might not have the merit of even one percent of the glorification but it is made to appear so on the Certificate. This 'Sehra' is no longer read aloud. Everything is calligraphed and engraved. It digs rather deep into those who don't receive it!

There is another form also. It's classified as 'Vaijayanti'... and is simply called 'Trophy.' It is almost like a 'Toffee' to console innocent kids. Sometimes literary writers are consoled by offering them 'Trophy.' It used to be in the form of a 'Shield.' 'Shield' or an armour. How far could a writer protect himself from being stripped off by a critic's cruelty? So, the 'Shield' became his refuge. Now the norms have undergone a sea-change. A writer can easily threaten even a fair, non-offensive critic. He is in no need of 'Shield' protection.

Another form of 'Trophy' is a 'Cup' which looks like a 'Wine-Glass.' All writers are fond of these types of 'Cups.' This form of Trophy is intoxicating. The honourable writer receives the 'Cup-Trophy' from the Chief Guest, just like a 'Wine Glass' from a Bar-Girl. The Cup presenter is like a detached Yogi. With a forced smile, he hands over the 'Trophy.' At times the photographer makes them repeat the give and take process again and again. Somehow the Chief Guest manages to deliver a better smile during repeat performance.

Some 'Trophies' are of special varieties or designer 'Trophies.' Most cherished is the one with an in-built clock. The moment when the writer receives that 'Trophy' is definitely lucky. But the luck soon fades away. They are a contractor's delight...over a span of 24 hours they stay unmoved and show correct time twice! That time gets stamped on them. This 'Trophy 'is symbolic of how the writer gets stamped by the Lucky Moment when the Trophy was handed over to him. Almost every writer who is rising, had arisen or has been repeatedly rising is in possession of one such mortal clock studded Trophy.

There are beautiful veiled Trophies in vogue these days. They lead the series of latest arrivals. They represent the marketing stunts and 'On popular demand' culture of ultra modernism...small or big, real or fake, any type of Trophy can be permanently set in boxes of high-quality transparent plastic sheets. Well protected from dust, the lady of the house also feels happy because it is easy to maintain it without any hassles and the writer husband also remains hassle free!

'Tamga' or Medals were also presented as token of respect since time immemorial. The prominent State level Awards are conferred in form of tiny medals in Palacial State Bungalows or President House. Gold Medals and Silver Medals are available in the market for a hundred rupees or eighty rupees respectively. They are woven in red, blue, yellow or green coloured ribbons to garland the writer.

Medal teaches us not to go on the price of anything. Try to assess its worth. Don't look at money, cherish the emotions and esteem associated with it. The ribbons used in the Medal also impart a lesson. They are indicative of the presenter's ideology—'Sanskar Bharati' uses saffron, Socialists use red, while Congress uses white ribbons. The height of its emotional flavour is almost like the cap adorned by the politicians on their head. The colour formula is applicable there also. They stand out in such prestigious 'Medal' conferring jubilations. The 'Medals' that appear to be small, can inflict grave injury to those who were in the race but did not make it to the list. It includes all medals designated as 'Shri,' whether it is 'Padma Shree' or 'Vyangya Shree.'

For the process of honouring, bouquet and garlands also add to the splendour of the programme. At unfavourable times, only a flower is presented. It is commonly seen that the honoured dignitaries intentionally leave the bouquet and garlands at the venue. These keep gracing or disgracing the place. Those who enjoy the honours can neither value *'Pushp ki abhilasha'* nor estimate the worth of *'Vanmali!'*

The garland is an expression of regards and greatness...many times one dignitary is overloaded with several of them...and when the garlands are in short supply for the next dignitary, it is taken off from the previous one and adorned around the neck of the next one...During this ceremony the 'Timing and Tuning' is magical. The momentum between 'You take off-You put it on' is seamless. The rise and fall of urgency is mind blowing.

In line with the tradition of commemoration the writer is coronated with a 'Tilak' of red paste on his forehead. Literary Coronation has stayed in practice despite the vanishing ritual of 'King's Coronation' and the fall of Royal-Dominions. Partly due to ignorance of the mannerism and idea behind 'Tilak' ceremony and partly due to euphoria, it is common to see the face and nose of the writer smeared in red. Thankfully, the paste is not black, otherwise...!

Lately, a novel style of citation has come up in literary circles. Getting a membership of an Academy is considered a laudable achievement. In the hoopla and strife to get membership, some petty writers forsake their dignity and become shallow sycophants. They get into the Academy hoping to be considered suitable for quick Awards. They get clicked with Ministers and other prominent celebrities during premium parties. They use these pictures to create a hype on the social media and then to further their interest they submit their resignation from the Academy on the pretext of some evitable or inevitable reason. Now their short-cut to become eligible for an Award is wide open. Side by side a treasure house also becomes available to them. The Academy members are not entitled to receive any Awards, so as soon as they resign, their chances to be Awarded become bright. The perfect Modus Operandi to secure an Award is to get Academy Membership, Grow Contacts and Encash an Award!

In our country, the crisis is that the number of writers is less while the Awards are more. The tried and tested formula in Private Sector is that 'You give us donation and we will confer you with a glorious Award.' There are numerous organisations to provide you with a spree of Awards while you 'Stay at Home'! For struggling writers an ever-expanding platform is available where you can rise from 'India's Who's Who,' to 'Asia's Who's Who' to 'World's Who's Who'! Opening wider and wider like the Mouth of Monster *'Sursa,'* you can pay a fee according to the level you wish to achieve and get your name and work (?) entered. If your photo is to be included, pay a little more...not only this, you can refer three more names to these Institutions and Organisations for similar services. If you remain oblivious to the 'Trap in their

Trade' you might be offered a reasonable concession on your Entrance Fee!

O somnolent writers, take a look! Awards are littered all around you...like desperation, dignity of poor, tantrums of a politician! Wake up and reach out for them. You do not know the Honour you deserve. Awake and make a sincere effort. Reward someone and be Awarded!

An Honour is your prestige. Honour gives life to your Biodata. It shows your worth. If you feel something is turning in you, dripping in you, sighing in you, realize that your soul is yearning for an Award and applaud. Don't care for anything else, leave aside all ego, by hook or by crook find an Award and become famous!

So what if you have not written songs to inspire anyone, if your friends are no good, if the literary world is not in awe of you. A writer is nothing without an Honour. If you are not a philosopher, it doesn't matter; fetch an Honour and become Eminent. If anything hurts your soul, go ahead and return The Award. You have understood that Honour begets Honour-This is the Eternal Postulate...! When you let the soul sleep and receive an Award, it becomes a single column news and when the soul gets suddenly shaken up, and you return the Award, it becomes three column news.

Now the ball is in your court. It is up to your Destiny and Karma that how many columns News you can be...so Arise, Awake, Decide and be Honoured!

□

24
Me Too Horror

I am horrified for past few days. Due to surge of 'Me Too' episodes, male ego of all men is at risk. Those few faded memories when weak moments boosted us, flash back time and again...We no longer recollect the fair and lovely faces of the damsels we managed to touch with twisted dramatics on the pretext of accidentally knocking against them, but we do remember our sleazy gestures... Memories of those whose shoulders or back we stroked with our rough hands are now giving us a bad taste... how those vulgar intentions developed at a rapid pace and while caught in their grip, how we arranged to meet them in private. All those thoughts keep churning our mind... Those who had to bear all that indecency, have now earned name and fame. Their gigantic images haunt us in imagination, so much so that we can't even sleep... we are always afraid that they might trap us in a 'Me Too' scandal. How we allured some of them at the pretence of offering a job and then got a good feel of them...and like wise! Whenever those past happenings seem come alive...another parallel thought also springs up...How happy and carefree must be the one who shared a juicy book with us in our adolescence and assured us that if we didn't understand something, she would help. There was another one, who had said after the interview, that if selected, she would always keep us happy...and many more!!! Nay, they would not even remember that we once existed in their life.

There is one big concession in the 'Me Too' process. We are not considered a celebrity but might be there is a high-profile lady who will disclose our past lewd behaviour and thereby make us a celebrity! We will at least have a name, even if for unchaste reasons. Just like 'Me Too,' there should have been a 'He Too' also. Then we would not have been so much horrified and those damsels would not have scared us with so much hue and cry!

□

25

Might is Not Right

Some of the youngsters like us were preparing for Civil Services Exams. Last Monday we planned to discuss 'Gulf War between America and Iran' with Professor Chiman Lalji but we were told that he had left for Mumbai.

Suddenly on Saturday he could be located twittering in Majlis. There was a hullabaloo. After putting the personal concerns to rest, he invited queries on the topics of General Knowledge. He was in a mood to answer it all. As usual we made friendly gestures and offered him a seat in the middle with peanuts, gajjak and tea.

Prof. Chiman Lal solemnly placed a bite of gajjak in his mouth and said, 'Friends, before we talk about the reality of Gulf listen to the folklore from Mumbai, otherwise I might forget it.'

We were all ears and listened to his broadcast (Enjoy the episode in his words)

'Friends, Mumbai is a city of Co-operative Housing. People, take Membership and then inhabit in their respective flats in these houses. The flat of the 'Bhai' I stayed with, was in a Co-operative House where mighty Tara Pehalwan and little Munnu Babu lived.

Tara Pehalwan was fond of having pet-dogs. He was

interested in puppies more than the dogs. His puppies always stayed like that. They didn't grow up. Munnu Babu felt like keeping one of his puppies with himself. That puppy was very fluffy and cute. It is said that Munnu's father once had that puppy and he gifted it to Tara Pehalwan. Munnu Babu was the youngest member of the Co-operative while Tara Pehalwan was heavy built, huge and mighty strong. He was very well off and was liberal in money matters.

One day Munnu picked up that puppy of Pehalwan and decided to take it to his house. After all it belonged to his father! Munnu Babu was a unique character, fearless and courageous. He liked taking risks. He had been having long standing conflicts with his neighbours and had become obsessive and strong headed. Hr got so fascinated with that puppy that he replaced the collar provided by Pehalwan with his own collar. Then he took it to his house and started playing and fiddling with it. The puppy started making uneasy noises. Pehalwan happened to hear them.

Pehalwan followed the voice and tried to find where his dear puppy was. He came to know from Dayaram that Munnu had taken it away. Dayaram told him that he tried to stop Munnu from doing so, but he did not listen.

Pehalwan reached Munnu's house. He started cajoling the puppy from outside his house. Munnu outrightly refused to return the puppy. After all it did not belong to Pehalwan's father.

It was but natural for Pehalwan to lose his temper. He started yelling out and calling him names. He dared him to come out and confront him. On hearing the commotion several members of the society came out to see what the matter was. Some tried to make Munnu understand the problem, but it was a futile exercise. Some were extremely happy at the tussle because there was someone who could take on Pehalwan! Pehalwan was bent upon of grabbing Munnu. He prepared to break into the flat with the intention of thrashing him. That's when Mathur Saab, Dayaram Gokhale and Gavaskar tried to intervene. They tried to reason out with him that he was a mature person while Munnu was just a kid. Won't it be shameful on his part to beat a child. With so much of resistance, Pehalwan went back. Friends, many people advised Munnu to return the puppy but Munnu was in no mood to relent. Ultimately the matter came to the notice of the Working Committee of the Society. An Emergency Session was convened wherein it was decided that Munnu should be given the custody of the Puppy for 3 days during which he should fullfil his desire to play with the puppy and then give it back to Pehalwan. Otherwise Pehalwan can take whatever action as his choice.

Munnu was anyway thinking that the puppy belonged to him. Three days passed. Even on fourth day puppy was not returned. Pehalwan lost his patience. He picked his practice 'Mudgar' and rushed towards Munnu's flat, threatening him of dire consequences. Anxious society members were peeping out of their windows. 'Now Munnu will be made to bite the dust'...they all were apprehensive. A few were happily waiting to see how Munnu will get punished for being cheeky.

Mathur Saab mocked at the raging Pehalwan, 'Oh, you would use such weaponry against a petty flea? He is just a little boy and you are taking such a heavy rod to hit him?'

Tara dropped his Mudgar. Mathur Saab was a journalist. He had got Tara's pictures published on two occasions. Hearing his voice Pehalwan cooled down. He dashed to Munnu's flat and started knocking against it with full force. The door neither opened nor broke down. He had not expected that the door would be so strong.

Society members were also surprised to see such bold and stubborn attitude of Munnu. Pehalwan then brought a piece of rock and started banging the door with it. Slowly, the door started giving way. That's when Munnu hurled Tara Pehalwan with water filled balloons from his terrace. The water was mixed with a chemical which made Tara itchy all over. His eyes started burning.

This infuriated the Mighty Man. Full of feelings of anger, insult and revenge, he rushed back to his home. He used some medications and returned to Munnu's house with his Dumbells, Practice Mudgur and stick. Everyone was watching intently. Now Munnu was hiding in the basement. Pehalwan was not able to break through the roof of the basement...after all German cement was used in making it!

Pehalwan returned once again and called his friend Pehalwan on phone. Society members were surprised to see that afterall, the Pehalwan was not a really mighty pehalwan. How come he had failed to get hold of even a small-fry like Munnu Babu?

On the other hand, Munnu played a new trick. He started throwing those poisonous balloons on other Society Members. Now the neighbours pleaded with Pehalwan, 'Leave Munnu alone. It's just a matter of a puppy...get another one!'

Tara Pehalwan was upset. He could not think of a way

out. His friend from practice ring had also arrived and marched towards Munnu's flat with a lot of hullabaloos. Everyone had only one thing on their mind-Come what may, Munnu has to be taught a lesson! When he can steal Tara's puppy, he can steal anything from anyone else!

Munnu felt that now he was trapped and will lose in the brawl. He wanted to win at all cost. He thought for a moment and then jumped from one terrace to the other. It had a huge water supply tank. He threatened that if anyone will trouble him or ask for the puppy, he would contaminate the water supply.

Everyone was in for a shock. All big cities are in short supply of water. Where will they get drinking water? What about bathing and cleaning?

Now everyone was after Tara Pehalwan and requested him to leave Munnu alone. Why trouble the lad. The puppy did not belong to him, anyway...etc.

All the pehalwan present there felt their body had gone listless. What could be done next? They started abusing Munnu. Suddenly in an effort to open the tank, Munnu broke it away.

With the bursting of the tank, thousands of gallons of water gushed out and...!'

Chiman Lal Bansal left the story at this juncture, unceremoniously! He took deep breaths and started sipping his cup of tea. We lost patience and asked, what happened next? What did Pehalwan do?'

'Was Munnu beaten up? Did the flat give way?'

'Professor, what happened finally?'

'The matter must have come to the notice of residents of Mumbai. What did people say?'

So many questions were shooting like missiles

towards Chiman Lalji, but he was cool like Saddam Hussein. After he finished his cup of tea, he said, 'Under the pressure of water the cooing puppy fell off on the head of Pehalwan standing below. Munnu Babu also fell unconscious after falling off. Since then, Pehalwan is having a persistent headache. He still rears puppies but now they do not remain puppies-they become lions! He has lost the 'Might is Right' attitude he once enjoyed.'

'So, the story is now over. Now you may ask anything about Gulf-War. You wanted to know the details of America and Iran relationship? I am ready for political discussion."

We were waiting for several weeks to ask so many questions from Professor. For some unknown reason we could neither ask anything nor utter a single word. We had found all correct answers!

□

26
Genius Cat

A cat stood in front of a truck on the main road. The truck was loaded with sugarcane. She said 'Driver-driver, stop the truck.' The truck driver stopped and asked, 'What do you want?' The cat said, 'I have to build a house with walls and roof for my kittens. First give me some sugarcane for that. 'The truck driver obliged and gave her some of his sugarcane.'

On the third day the cat was again on the road. A truck full of jaggery came that way. She managed to get some jaggery from the truck driver so that she could stick together the walls and roof made of sugarcane shoots.

After three days she was again on the road. This time she took some rice to paste upon the house surface.

The cat did not use those three things to make a house. She consumed the juice of sugarcane, stored the jaggery and sold the rice in black.

Very next day the cat again blocked the road!!!

□

27

University Shraadh Season—A Screenplay

Opening scene shows a ringing telephone with zoom in from long shot to close up. A hand picks up the receiver and a voice is heard.

Voice: Hello, hello Professor Chiman speaking. Yes? I am Prof. Chiman speaking.

Cut to—

The camera moves to long shot where Prof. Chiman is seen speaking on phone.

Prof. Chiman: 'Oh yes! Mr. Ahuja you have called after such a long time. Oh, you were thinking about me! Thank you, thank you. Yes, your Bhabhi is doing well. Our daughter is also well. She is in seventh now.

Oh, what are you saying! You are my fan? Oh, we are all friends! You are there in my thoughts also. If you feel like seeing me, just drop in...

...no formality, come over...what?

You are coming? You are already here?'

He happily puts the receiver on the cradle and turns back. He finds Mr. and Mrs. Ahuja knock at the door and enter. Mrs. Ahuja has a box of sweets in her hands while Mr. Ahuja is holding his mobile.

Cut to—

Chiman: Oh Mr. Ahuja wonderful! You called from just outside my house? Namastey Bhabhi!

Mr. and Mrs. Ahuja: Namastey

Cut to—

Mr. Ahuja comes up to Prof. Chiman and hugs him. Gladly they make themselves comfortable on the sofa as Prof. Chiman welcomes them.

Cut to—

Looking inside,

Chiman: Just see Sudha, who has come!

Cut to—

The frame shows Mr. and Mrs. Ahuja having tea with Mr. Chiman and laughing together.

Cut to—

Prof. Chiman: Mr. Ahuja, you were in Ajmer. Have you got transferred here?

Ahuja: No no, we have come from Ajmer to see you!

Chiman: Just for me? Really??

Mrs. Ahuja: He was getting impatient. For three days he was saying that he was very keen to see you. He even got his old album. He showed me all the College Day photographs and said 'Just see, how smart Chiman Bhai looked even then!'

(Prof. Chiman smiles shyly)

Ahuja: My friend is still so handsome. He must be always surrounded by girl students! Am I not right Bhabhiji?

Mrs. Chiman: Oh, Bhai Saheb, that was long back. Now he has become wise. But I wonder how could you really walk all the way from Ajmer...just to meet us! We are really impressed.

Ahuja: No no, we haven't walked all the way...we came in our old worn-out car. It took us full eight hours. We started at 4 in the morning. I couldn't get even a wink of sleep. I kept thinking about you.

Chiman: Ahuja tell me, how are your children? Where are they? You didn't bring them with you?

Ahuja: Children! You know I got married as soon as I got my job. You were busy with your MA and PhD...

(In between)

Chiman: I am asking about children and you...

Ahuja: Yes, I was coming to that-my son Ashish is appearing for his twelfth exams and Shikha has appeared for tenth exams...both had Board Exams.

Chiman: You should have...Oh, so they are busy with their exams! You could have come after the exams and brought them along...

Ahuja: When I was hungry now, how could I keep waiting for three days? I felt like flying down to meet you. So we just came over leaving them behind. My mother is there with them. Their next exam is after three days and that is the last one.

Chiman: Sudha, arrange for their lunch now. It's past 2 O' Clock...they left at four in the morning...they have travelled such a long distance for us...both of you get refreshed, we will get lunch served in the meantime!

Mrs. Ahuja: Bhai Sahib, we had meals at the border only. We reached at 1. The dhaba had hot lunch ready. You just be comfortable...we have had tea...now we will return shortly.

Chiman: Return? So early? Did you come all the way just to show your faces?

(Feeling sad)

Ahuja: No no, Ashish was saying just go and come back...that...that...

Shila, you tell...that...

(Mrs. Ahuja hints him to continue further...)

Cut to—

Mrs. Chiman and Prof. Chiman look at each other and acknowledge one another' smile.

Mrs. Chiman: Prof. Sahib...Shraadh are about to begin. The days of Kanagat are about to come, Crows will get kheer to enjoy...tararrum!

(Both start laughing)

Mr. and Mrs. Ahuja look at them confused

Ahuja: Shraadh? What's that about? Crows...I don't get it!

Chiman: Oh, why don't you tell yourself what your son who is in twelfth said...? Shraadh is our personal matter, between me and Sudha. What did your son say?

Mrs. Chiman:...that I should get admission in Chiman Uncle's College. So, do some buttering, get them some sweets...

Cut to—

(Uneasy looking Ahuja couple in frame)

Ahuja: You know...actually the matter is...whom else will we tell if not you?...you have to find and get him admission in your College. You are in the Head position.

(Hints to Mrs. Ahuja to say something)

Mrs. Ahuja: Yes Bhai sahib, he wanted to meet you since long...

(Laughing in between)

Mrs. Chiman: But the son has now come to twelfth class...O Shila, you could have said at the outset that you have come for your son' s admission...even we started thinking that you had come to meet us from such a long distance!

Ahuja: Oh...Chiman Bhai, do I look like a crow...though I know my complexion is a little dark!

Chiman: Ahuja, you are a swan...actually it's me who is a crow. Now I will have a great time for around two months. The fact is that these are going to be Shraadh days in the university. Those who are chased away from the terrace all the year round, those who made to shut their mouth as soon as they try to speak, those crows will now have a good time. The devotees will invite them with all benevolence and offer them sweet savoury dishes...you still didn't get it, my devotee, Mr. Ahuja? We the lecturers in colleges, who are called Professors are like the crows of Shraadh. Admission days are like Shraadh days. For the satisfaction of our forefathers, we feed the crows, similarly we are...

(Laughs. Mr. and Mrs. Ahuja get up dazed and fold their hands)

Ahuja: Namastey Bhabhi! Bye Professor! We will make a move. Children must be waiting. We will come again...

(Fade out)

(Fade in)

Same room. Chiman and his wife are relaxing on the sofa.

Mrs. Chiman: 'When did you start thinking about theses crows? Since the time I got married, you used to say at the beginning of every summer vacation that let us leave for Shimla or Mussouri, otherwise the Shraadh people will come. They will not go till they get their share.'

Chiman: 'Sudha, when I got married, I was already teaching in a college for six years. I was a bachelor and stayed in a rented room in a colony. I was a strange creature for the colony women who sit on the charpoys outside their doors.'

Cut to—(Flashback)

Scene of a colony where some women are sitting on a charpoy and gossiping. One of them is knitting a sweater. The other one is peeling some seeds. Looking into the camera two of them feel scared and in the closeup, two of them are seen talking to each other.

One woman: 'Oops, there he comes.'

Second: 'He has grown his beard. He dresses up in suit, lives in style, rogue looking boys come to meet him...'

First: 'Even girls are also seen visiting him. They keep uttering Sirr Sirr...all the time...'

Second: 'Just see, how upright he walks. Let me shift my charpoy inside.'

First: 'Let me also shift inside...look, he is here!'

Cut to—

Well suited booted young Chiman Lal come walking with a serious expression and walks past the camera. His back is seen.

Cut to—The previous two women are in frame.

First: 'He does not look like one, but he is definitely some thief, dacoit or as they show in films...smuggler.'

Second: Smuggler...'Do you know, I have seen, many times at night, lights can be seen through his open window. That lady from house number four was saying that he teaches in a college...is a professor there. Keeps reading and writing the whole of the night. That's why his light remains on. I can't make out whether he is a thief or a decent guy.'

Cut to—

First scene

Prof. Chiman and his wife are sitting on the sofa and talking.

Mrs. Chiman: 'Then they ultimately got to know the truth about you.'

Chiman: 'You know Sudha crow is a very unique bird...very alert, very clever. But no one likes it...when the women got sure that I am a decent professor, the women did not pick up the charpoy...but remained careful.'

Mrs. Chiman: 'Why?'

Chiman: 'That is because everyone knows that a crow can be dangerous but in reality, it is not so. Just give him a hint with your hand and it will immediately fly away.

...so, they remained careful that it might not become dangerous.'

Sudha: 'So no one spoke to you?'

Chiman: 'Yes, they did, that's how I came to know about the days of Shraadh...I had shifted there for four months...while I was passing through the colony with head bent down...'

Cut to—Flashback

Chiman is walking through the colony with a bent head. Suddenly a female voice is heard...

Voice: 'Sir, Namastey Sir.'

Cut to—

Chiman looks into the camera with a bent head and smiles

Cut to—

A beautiful girl comes into frame. She folds her hands.

Girl: 'Sir, my mother is calling you home.'

Girl indicates to the right side.

Chiman looks that side. A woman in her forties is

standing there with folded hands...camera pans that woman.

Woman: 'Namastey Professor Sahib! Please visit our house today, your feet will purify it.'

Cut to—

Prof. Chiman looks alarmed and gaze towards his feet.

Cut to—

Dirty shoes are seen

Cut to—

Chiman tries to swallow and moves on.

Cut to—

The girl and the woman indicate towards the door of the house.

Cut to—

Next scene

Chiman is sunk in the drawing room sofa. The woman is slowly waving a hand fan to make him comfortable. The girl is standing with a samosa plate next to him. Several sweets and other dishes are set on the centre table.

Woman: 'Please have samosa, Professor Sahib. We are lucky that today you have come to our house.'

'You are highly educated. I told my husband several times to invite you home...but he is so busy with his business and minting money...please have something... Give him...'

(The girl picks up the plate and offers him. Chiman picks up a samosa like an obedient child.)

Chiman: 'Yes yes...I will take. You are very nice people. Actually, I live alone here. I don't know anyone in the Colony...just my students happen to come at times to see me or study from me. I will surely come to your place Baby...'

Woman: 'Call her Dolly...She is Dolly...'

(Enthusiastically)

Chiman: 'Whenever Dolly' s daddy is at home, I will come and see him.'

Woman: 'Dolly's daddy? He hardly knows what is happening at home. Now just see, Dolly had cleared her twelfth...but he hardly knows how to get her admitted to a college...it's all my responsibility. But how do I know which course is good for her...all this has to be decided by you.'

Chiman: 'Me?'

Woman: 'Whichever College she will go to...you only will get her admitted in.'

Chiman: 'Me?'

Woman: 'Who else, if not you! You know, I can't! Everything has to be done by you. My husband does not pay any attention to her. You have to give her all your attention.'

Chiman: 'My attention?'

Woman: 'Yes yes, I consider you more than my husband. A good neighbour is more than a close relative. In the whole of the world the only one who can take care of my daughter is either God or you...Professor Sahib, besides you, there is no one else.'

Cut to—

Chiman tastes sweets in silence.

Cut to—

Crows taste offerings.

Cut to—

Prof. Chiman feels happy and enjoys himself

Cut to—

Crows are hopping and making merry.

Cut to—

The woman and the girl serve more plates.

Cut to—Woman and girl put bowls full of milk in front of the crow.

Cut to—

The crow flies away.

Cut to—

Prof. Chiman comes out of the woman's house.

Cut to—

(Previous scene)

Mrs. Chiman is having a fit of laughter.

Mrs. Chiman: 'Now I know the history of your Crow episode...that's why as soon as the last part of the summer vacation begins, you and your devotees get ready...but your devotees hardly remember you after it's all over...'

Chiman: 'Sudha, after the Kanagat days are over, till the completion of Shraadh, people forget the crows also... this is the time cycle. The crow also does not bother...next time Shraadh will come again, crow will again eat to his heart's content...might be some time his beak gets cast in gold...

(Both laugh. The doorbell rings and someone calls)

Chiman: 'Who is there?'

Voice: 'At your service Professor Chiman Bhai, I am Radheylal.'

(Chiman and Mrs. Chiman look at each other and Mrs. Chiman says with a soft smile)

Mrs. Chiman: 'Get ready, there comes the one who would get the golden beak...'

(Chiman looks on with a hilarious expression)

Freeze

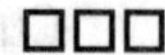